The Rat Race

By

Sara Logan

ISBN-13: 978-0-9854186-0-1

ISBN-13: 978-0-9854186-1-8 (e-book)

Many thanks to Miles, for all of his support.

"Here's your mail, sir." The guy from the mail room dropped a crate on the table just inside of the editor's office. The crate was filled, as usual, with bulky envelopes full of manuscripts for his consideration.

"Thanks, Ed. Have a good one." The editor continued on with the manuscript he was reviewing, snorted, and stuffed it back into the accompanying self-addressed, stamped envelope along with a pro-forma rejection letter. *Another crummy story*, he thought. *Folks keep sending in flowery language dressing up hollow stories. Maybe I should get back into real estate.* He glanced at the clock. 2:37 in the afternoon. His eyes strayed to the new crate of manuscripts. Sighing, he walked over to the table and pulled out several envelopes. He shredded open the first and began reading the cover letter.

"Enclosed for your consideration is my semi-autobiographical novel detailing a girl's traumatic coming of age..." he read, then threw the manuscript into the REJECT pile. Next was a really thick packet, the manuscript covered with a cover letter and a cover page boldly proclaiming Word Count 172,947. "Thank you for taking the time to read my first novel. I've been working on it for two years. My junior high English teacher thinks it is grate. I think you are grate too." REJECT. Next package, cover letter in a heavy, angular font. "Four thousand years into the future, my protagonist accidentally falls into a timewarp and is sent back into the 1960s. After landing in a group of hippies in the middle of the Sonoran desert, he drops acid and hallucinates that his life in the future is nothing but a dream..." REJECT. *I should definitely get back into real estate*, he thought. *Anything would be better than acting as a filter for bad literature. I should get a public service award.* He pulled out another envelope, this one hard and lumpy. The return address said, "From the 99%." He snorted again.

The editor tugged the envelope open, and out fell a black and white composition notebook. No cover letter was enclosed. On the cover of the notebook was scrawled, "Want to hear the tale of how my life went to shit? Read on." He sat back down at his desk, flipped open the notebook, and began to read the first page, handwritten in tight, small, all-Caps ink.

* * * *

November 2007

My life was perfect. I had a growing career in a great job, working as a middle manager in a large insurance company. I was married to a great wife, who was both beautiful and intelligent, with a great job of her own. We were the archetypal DINKYs—double income, no kids yet. We had just built a custom home in a new community, with a Jacuzzi tub in the master bath, granite kitchen countertops and stainless steel appliances. Our lawn was trimmed once a week by a lawn service. Our house was cleaned twice a week by maid service. Clothes were cleaned by the dry-cleaners. We kept our bodies healthy by exercising daily and eating high-quality organic fruits and vegetables, whole grains, wild-caught fish from pollution-free waters, and free-range, anti-biotic free meats. When I chose to sully my body, it was only with hand-rolled cigars and the best small-batch bourbons. Cars were washed in the parking garages at our jobs while we sat up in our offices, taking care of business. We took cruises and vacationed in the islands. And I drove an awesome car, a BMW 535i. Life was sweet.

Then, it all went to shit.

January 2008

The first thing to go was my wife. I came home one day and did the usual—poured out some organic, wild-yeast chardonnay while she chopped vegetables to prepare dinner. "Funniest thing happened today," I said. I took a sip of the wine. Crisp, fruit-forward, with a lingering taste of melon and pear on my palate.

"Oh?" she asked. "What's that?" Chop. Chop. Chop. "Ow!" she cried, sucking her fingertip. "Danny, can you get me a bandaid?" I laughed.

"Can you cook a meal without putting a digit in it?" I got her a bandaid and an alcohol swab. She cleaned herself up, gave me a dirty look, and kept chopping the vegetables.

"Maybe if you would help me with the dinner..." she hinted. "Maybe if your contribution to dinner went beyond pouring the drinks...? Never mind. What happened?"

"That new guy quit. Remember I told you about him? Anderson? Everyone figured he wasn't really catching on very well. He wouldn't ask questions but he couldn't get his work done right. A little scary. Anyway, at lunch he asked the guy in the next cube what floor IT was on."

"That's not that funny. Everyone has IT problems every now and then." Lacey sounded a little bit bitter. She's not the most technologically savvy person, and spends a fair amount of time asking IT basic questions at work. She even has the IT department swap out her Blackberry whenever it's time for an upgrade. Like it's *sooooo* hard to sync a SIM card... but anyway.

"I didn't get to the funny part yet. The funny part was, then he went to IT, turned in his computer, left for lunch, and never came back." I sipped more wine. Yummy.

"That was it? Did he say anything? Like mention that he was quitting? Hey, can you pour me some wine, too? And set the table."

"Why do we have to eat at the table every night? There's only the two of us. We could eat around the breakfast bar." Lacey rolled her eyes at me as I poured some wine for her. "No, he never said anything to anyone. He just left. It wasn't going well for him anyway, he couldn't ever get his numbers to come out right. Said something about the spreadsheets showing losses, funny numbers that wouldn't tie out, stuff like that, and he was getting some heat from management about that. We all know that the company can't possibly be in losses."

Lacey leaned on the granite counter and sipped some wine. "Never said anything, huh? Just left." She stared into her wine glass. "Just left."

"Yeah, kooky shit, right?" I laughed. We ate dinner, and I watched the Redskins lose on Monday Night Football while Lacey washed the dishes and ran laundry.

The next day, Lacey left.

Her lawyer served the papers.

I had just come home from work, when the doorbell rang. I walked up and opened the door, and there he was, stuffiness in a suit. Who the hell knows why he served those papers in person, when he could have had an intern or a process server do it for him. Maybe his billable hours were low, and he needed more work. Maybe he wanted to get his vampire eyes on my house, figure out what it was worth, so that he would have personal knowledge of how much blood he could suck from my very veins. Maybe he wanted to verify that Lacey was not living in the home. I've come to learn that it takes a hell of a lot of effort and apart time to accomplish a divorce in the Commonwealth of Virginia, and if an estranged spouse decides to move back in, that can start the clock all over again. Well, he saw my house with just me living in it.

"Daniel?" He harrumphed, clearly uncomfortable. It was dark out, and he was huffing white puffs of condensation with each exhalation. He was dressed in a dark, sober suit, Republican Red tie, and the ubiquitous black wool dress coat that 97% of Washingtonians wear from November to February.

"How can I help you?" I asked.

"I'm here to deliver divorce papers from your estranged wife, Lacey. Please sign here," he stated, offering a clipboard and an envelope. I stared silently past him, noticing for the first time that little flecks of paint were peeling from the posts and rails on my front porch and steps. I don't know how I saw that in the dark, but the image froze with me. I can close my eyes and still pull up my precise stream of consciousness in that moment. Life is not perfect. Lacey is divorcing me. And I need to get the painters out here.

Of course I signed and took the papers. The lawyer went on his way. I didn't know what to do, so for a while I ignored the problem. After a couple of weeks, I shifted gears and got more proactive, seeking Lacey out, trying to re-engage her in our relationship. Maybe if I could figure out the issues she was facing, I would win her back, right? Unfortunately, I couldn't get anything out of Lacey for the longest time—she didn't tell me where she moved to, and she wouldn't answer my calls on her cell phone or at her job. Fortunately, her lawyer had stapled his card to the front of the business-sized envelope that contained the legal demise of my marriage. After a few testy messages back and forth, I finally got her lawyer to convey that I would contest the divorce, drag it out, unless she agreed to talk to me on the phone.

March 2008

Lacey agreed to one five-minute call. At the appointed time, I dialed her number, and she finally answered me.

"Lacey? Hey, Lacey. How are you?"

"Fine. Great."

"I miss you. Why don't you come home? Why don't we talk this over?"

"Forget it, Danny. I'm very glad that I left, and I don't think I want to see you again."

"But why?" I stuttered. "WHY? Our life is perfect!"

"No, Daniel, our lives are not perfect," she replied. "You just think it is. You and your juvenile little mind, driving around in your phallic-symbol car and listening to your dumb sports radio shows."

"My sports radio show is the cause of our divorce? What's wrong with sports radio? Those guys on the morning show are hilarious!"

"That's the trouble," she said. "You think those dopes are hilarious. After you got your degree, you turned off your brain outside of work. You never think anymore. You just want to have a good time listening to guys talk about sports, women and gambling—you, the guy who doesn't play sports, has no idea what to do with women, and never gambles. You live vicariously through the little boys on the morning show. I'm bored with you and bored with our lives. I'm appalled that I got a masters' degree so that I could work all day long at my job and then come home and take care of you, as though I'm your mommy. I want to check out from our marriage, check out from the rat race and focus on my art."

I snorted audibly. Lacey has always been convinced that she is an artist. She putters around in a local pottery studio on the weekend, making huge chunky plates that she hand-paints and attempts to sell for over $100 each, in the window of the studio. They get about one foot-traffic inquiry per day. In three years, she has sold two plates. I always told her I liked the plates, but quitting a job and divorcing a husband to go make 5-pound platters was just ludicrous.

"I knew that you never supported my art!" She exploded. "That just confirms that I'm right to leave. Goodbye, Daniel.

You'll be hearing from my lawyer about my share of the house."

Well, that was it. There was no talking her out of the divorce. I never could accept that we split up over my morning sports radio program or her f-ugly platters. I'm sure it was just a pretext, or transference, or some other term I could learn on the therapist's couch. Regardless, our marriage was over and she was gone. I started eating out at Clyde's every night. From home-cooked, organic meals to cocktails and steaks wasn't such a bad switch, although dinner alone was costing me $50 to $75 per night. I wondered how much my groceries used to cost. We always shopped at Whole Foods, joking that it should be called "Whole Paycheck", but I never paid attention to how much the groceries cost. Well, it cost what it cost, right? A man's gotta eat. I missed having company, but didn't necessarily miss the crap she would have given me over eating corn-fed beef and GMO produce. But she was right—I DID hear from her lawyer about the house.

April 2008

"She wants HOW MUCH?"

"One hundred twenty five thousand dollars. You maintained separate careers, separate bank accounts, separate car loans, and separate retirement portfolios, but you did commingle assets in the purchase of your home. I believe you initially purchased the home for $525,000. Your current mortgage balance is just under $500,000. And a similar home just sold in your neighborhood for $750,000. Lacey would like to sell the home and split the proceeds. Alternatively, you may buy her out for $125,000."

"But I couldn't afford to refinance the house to get that kind of cash out! I wouldn't qualify for the mortgage on just my income alone. She can't force me to sell the house, can she?"

Lacey's lawyer cleared his throat and looked down at the papers he was shuffling in his hands. Then he looked back up at me. "Look," he said, avoiding my eyes, "I can't really give you legal advice. I represent your estranged wife. But I really would recommend that you hire a lawyer and get a little help here. You don't want to go through a divorce without legal representation."

I took his advice and hired a lawyer. My buddy, Joe, from college had gone on to law school, and then hung out his shingle as a solo practitioner. He mostly did personal injury, but agreed to take on my case as a favor. Unfortunately for me, he didn't have much experience in divorce law, and was unable to get Lacey to drop her number. Ultimately, I took a loan out of my 401(k) account to pay her off, and the house was mine alone. The good news was, I owned the house and Lacey no longer had a claim on it. Although the house didn't make up for the sudden and inexplicable end to my marriage, at least I hadn't lost my wife and my house in the same transaction.

August 2008

The bad news was, a few months after taking out that 401(k) loan, the stock market went into the crapper and I was left with a net negative balance on my 401(k). Yep, that's right. The outstanding loan on my retirement account was more that the account was worth.

It's really no fun at all to open up that benefits page online to see the net value of a portfolio in the negative. I had been allowed to borrow up to 50% of my 401(k), and so I was able to get Lacey her $125,000 and still had another $125,000 in the 401(k) when I took out the loan, but when the market dropped, my account lost value from $250,000 down to $97,000. That left me almost $30,000 in the hole on my loan. Even worse, most of my 401(k) was invested in company stock, which had not fared too well when the market dipped. My chest tightened up, and I had to suck in a deep breath and blow it out slowly just to avoid an on-the-spot panic attack.

"Keep it together," I said to myself. *It's just a dip. It will rebound.* "Dollar-cost averaging," I said to myself. "This just means that equities are on sale right now. It will be ok. You'll pick up stocks for a bargain until the market picks up again!"

Yeah, I drank the Kool-Aid. I really believed all of that crap. Human Resources had brain-washed me with their slick benefits pamphlets, with pictures of smug executives on the cover in their LL Bean sweaters, looking casual and relaxed as they strolled around their country retreats on a fall weekend. Pour your money into the system, little person! they said to me. If you and 200 million other little people dump your money into the system, we can pay ourselves $10 million bonuses even if it all goes south.

Have no fear, I kept it together. I didn't freak out that day, or the next day, or the next. I patiently waited, confident, knowing that for my next 100 paychecks, or however long it took for the market to rebound, I would be able to buy stocks "at a discount!" through my regular 401(k) contributions, and ultimately benefit from what seemed to be a short-term crisis.

Time to tighten the belt, though--I switched from eating out at Clyde's to eating take-out rotisserie chicken dinners from Harris Teeter. That, and a bottle of Yellowtail wine every now and then, or some Robert Mondavi. They tasted alright, and were on sale in the wine section. That's right, I was rockin' the Teet, hitting the Fresh Foods Market every night, getting some wine, cheese, and chicken. Keeping it healthy, keeping it real, I cut my costs and kept plugging along. My cool composure didn't do me any good in the long run. Obama didn't keep his promise to our country and the economy didn't recover. My company eventually announced that it was going to go through cost-cutting measures, to eliminate any fat in the budget and boost shareholder value.

October 2011

That's right. The next thing to go was my job. The day started out like any other work day. I drove my BMW 535i to my local Starbucks, and walked in with my environmentally-friendly, Venti-sized aluminum travel mug. Patiently, I stood in line behind some crappy mom with her two crappy kids. They were jumping around, bumping into me and the people ahead of them, asking for chocolate milk and touching all of the merchandise. Some people need to learn to learn to control their kids. Finally I got to order my Venti, decaf skim no-whip mocha. Ah! Perfection in a cup. The barista handed me the travel mug, and I walked out the door. No paper napkins needed. I'm environmentally friendly like that. Why kill the trees? I fired up my V6 and revved the engine a couple of times. Crappy mom and crappy kids were wandering out the doors, and I revved the engine one more time, just to watch them jump, startled at the noise. Ha ha!

I drove off towards the office, listening to my sports radio show. I don't care what Lacey has to say about these guys—dumb? No! Maybe a little immature, but they are really fucking funny and they've made a ton of cash. They just sit around, doing what they love, talking about sports and women. I think that would be the greatest job on the planet.

As I drove, I lifted my travel mug up to take my first sip of morning joe. Too bad joe decided to piss on me today. Gross, decaf skim no-whip mocha all over the front of my shirt! With no napkins to clean it up... I stared at my travel-mug. The top had been screwed back on slightly askew, and as a result, when I tipped it up to take a sip, coffee had leaked through the threaded top. Fucking baristas! The job of last resort for American incompetents. And it was a big day, too—quarterly reports were coming due to management, and we always draft haiku as headers for the quarterly reports.

If you don't know what a haiku is—well, neither did I, when I first started this job. Turns out that a haiku is a kind of Asian poetry. It's always a three-line poem. The first line has five syllables, the second line has seven syllables, and the third line has five syllables again. It's sometimes hard to capture the essence of quarterly performance in those seventeen syllables. It takes peaceful contemplation and perfect zen. Think bamboo plants, rice paper walls, and waterfalls, and you've got in mind what it takes to write a good haiku.

Shit, my zen was all thrown off by the coffee stain on my shirt, and the coffee smell following me around. Maybe that had something to do with what happened next. Bad Karma. I got into work and joined up with the guys. We all sat together in the team room, laptops ablaze, trying to come up with the perfect 17 syllables to capture and define performance over the previous quarter. I was in the midst of counting syllables on my fingers, when a mass e-mail pinged on everyone's screen. My buddy Toby opened it up, and hissed, "Oh Fuck. What a cluster fuck."

"Is that your middle line, Tobe?" I asked. "How did you lead into it?"

"No you dumbass. Read your e-mail. Oh, Jesus Christ, what am I going to tell my wife?"

I looked at my laptop screen, then reached down to tab into the e-mail without losing count on my fingers. The haiku popped up on my screen:

> Market bottomed out
> Oh, losses, losses, losses
> We have jobs no more.

The e-mail was from our CEO.

CHAPTER ONE

Our company pretty much dissolved—no government bailout for us—and became the subject of an active and highly publicized SEC investigation, and the biggest public failure since Lehman Brothers had collapsed. The press ridiculed the company as being "Almost Too Big To Fail", a catchphrase that became the pseudonym for the company name. Several of my coworkers were highly scrutinized by the government and the press. I had not been involved in any wrongdoing to my knowledge, and was glad to escape public scrutiny, but not before I went through several colon-cleansing conversations with my lawyer.

"If you didn't know about the losses and the cooked books, you're in the clear," Joe told me. "You knew nothing, right?"

"Right," I lamely agreed, squirming internally, wondering whether my story about the day Anderson quit demonstrated "knowledge" that the company was in losses.

Did I tell that story to anyone but Lacey? Would Lacey tell that story to the SEC? Would the SEC even think to talk to Lacey? We had been separated for years. Was I going to go to jail? Had I done anything wrong? Should I ask my lawyer these questions? "Look, Joe—if I tell you stuff, that's privileged, right? You can't tell anyone or testify against me, can you?" Silence over the phone. Then, I could hear a drawer opening and the sound of something rattling. "Joe?"

"Just grabbing some Tums, my good buddy," he said. "That's not my favorite client line of all times. Ok, yes, you can tell me anything you need to tell me, and I can't testify against you, but I really hope you don't have anything to tell me."

I explained to him the anecdote from the day Anderson quit. "Hmm," Joe said. "Did you review Anderson's work?"

"No," I said. "He mentioned that his numbers weren't tying out, they showed losses instead of gains, and that didn't make sense, since the workpapers I was working on showed gains, but I didn't review his work. I was using the numbers that Anderson's supervisor was feeding to me. I never checked Anderson's workpapers to see if they were the same number."

"That's ok then," said Joe. "If Anderson verbalized that his work showed that the company was in losses, but you didn't see any documentation to that effect, then his statement is just hearsay. It's not admissible. Unless you were actually involved in preparing the workpapers that disguised the losses, I'm not sure you really had knowledge. We'll have to see how this all shakes out with the SEC. Hang tight there, buddy. Besides, that isn't really the biggest issue you have right now."

"I'm sorry, what? Possible indictment and prison time isn't the biggest issue I have?"

"hahaha!" Joe chuckled happily. "Oh, don't worry, the SEC will save all of the prison time for the executives. The worse that you might get would be a hefty fine, around $25,000."

My innards clenched. "Joe, I have no money. Lacey just shook me down for every penny, I'm unemployed, and the company obviously has no cash for severance packages. I can't pay a fine like that."

"Oh, you don't have to tell me that. I know you're broke. I did your divorce settlement, remember? No, the biggest issue that you have right now is the money that you owe to Almost Too Big To Fail."

"What? The money that *I* owe?" My voice took on a shrill, unhappy tone. "How do I owe them money? I wasn't embezzling, if that's what they think!"

"Oh, no, of course not. This isn't any kind of accusation. Look, you had an active loan out on your 401(k) account, that you took out to pay off Lacey so that you can stay in your house. You know, to buy out her share of the equity. Anyway, the outstanding loan exceeds the balance of your 401(k). You're upside down. According to your company's HR policy, since you are now separated from the company, you have to immediately pay off the loan. You may have to liquidate your 401(k) to do so, and you may even still have an outstanding balance."

Ka·thump. Ka·thump. Ka·thump. In the silence, my heart was banging my chest wall like a jackhammer.

"Oh, and Danny, when you liquidate your 401(k), you owe federal taxes on the full amount withdrawn, and a 10% penalty on top of that. You know, the IRS has these rules. So I guess the IRS is your biggest worry right now. No problem. If you don't have the cash to pay the taxes on your 401(k) by next April, we'll file an extension on your taxes. That gives you until next October. So really, you have a year to come up with the money to pay your taxes."

"Joe, I can't believe it. Can they really make me do that?"

"On the bright side, they probably won't come after you for the outstanding amount. Just pay them what you can, and it will likely be ok. They probably won't come after you for a couple of years. This will all work its way out in the bankruptcy hearings."

Mine or the company's? Never mind. So that was that. I did as Joe advised, and liquidated my 401(k). I paid off as much of the loan as I could, but there was still thousands left that I still owed to my old company, and Joe correctly surmised that I owed a hefty bill to the IRS. Even worse, although I applied to all of the advertised jobs in the area that met my skills, and fired off over 100 unsolicited resumes, I wasn't getting calls for job interviews. I wasn't sure what was going on, until one day I called the hiring department of one of the advertised jobs. I talked to the recruiter and gave a vanilla version of my background. She was enthusiastic and scheduled me for an in-person interview. Then, I e-mailed over my resume. Ten minutes later, she e-mailed me back, letting me know that I wasn't the "right fit" for the job. I called her back.

"Penny, hey, it's Danny—we just talked? I thought we had an interview set up, you were interested—what happened?" I tried not to sound pathetic or desperate.

"Um, hi. Sorry. We've been asked not to hire anyone from Almost Too Big To Fail. You know, until the investigation is over. But good luck. Best of luck to you. Bye now. Bye bye." Penny hung up over my vague protestations.

I figured that, although I was bereft of savings (due to the divorce) and had no severance package, I could weather the storm by taking out a home equity line of credit. Worst case scenario, I would sell my house and take my share of the equity. Lacy had walked away with more than a hundred big, so why couldn't I? I could live off of that for a while, until I found a new job.

I called up my buddy, Larry, who is a primo real estate wheeler-dealer, to get his advice. What he had to tell me was a total shock.

"Look, Danny, about the house. Yeah, I don't think you should really sell the house."

"Larry, hey, thanks for calling me back. What's that? Don't sell? Look, if it's about investment horizons and long-term strategy, my horizon is immediate. I really need the money. I know that the house will keep appreciating, but I'm pretty short on liquid assets right now."

"Uh, right. No, see, the economic model for the market has been correcting over the past couple of years, okay? Given your particular data and the price point in the market, now is not the optimal time for you to exit."

"I don't follow. Correcting?" What was this guy talking about?

"Right. See, since your divorce, the market correction has resulted in a softened market, so now isn't the greatest time to consider selling."

"Look, Larry, I feel like you're losing me in the buzzwords. Can you just give me a straight answer? Why shouldn't I sell the house?"

"Long story short, Danny? You couldn't sell that house for what you paid for it. You're totally upside-down on your loan. In terms of the overall market, if you bought at $500K, you can count on selling at $415K. If you bought at $415K, you'll be selling at $350K. Nobody that bought or built a house in the past five years can get out what they paid for it. So unless you put down a hell of a lot of money, you are stuck in that house."

"Oh my God." I sat down hard. "How could this happen? I thought real estate always went up?"

"A lot of people thought that, Danny. And it turns out that a lot of banks wrote really shitty commercial paper, betting that real estate would always go up. Then, that shitty paper got rehashed into what looked like not-too-shabby securities, and went out on the open market. You should know all of this. Don't you work for that insurance company? Or I guess, you DID work for that insurance company, right? The one that was Almost Too Big To Fail?"

"I'm screwed. I'm screwed," I moaned. "I can't make my payments and I can't sell the house. I'm going to be out on the street, living out of a refrigerator carton. I'll be sleeping in my car. Oh God!"

"Hey, Danny, don't get so worked up," crooned Larry. "Look, buddy, it's going to be all right. The mortgage companies are doing so many foreclosures these days, it'll be months before they catch up with you. Maybe years. You won't be in risk of foreclosure until you miss a few months payments, and even if they started the process promptly it takes a while before they throw you outta the house. Look, you'll get another job before then, catch up on your payments, and you'll be fine."

"Oh, God. Maybe I should get my family to loan me some money, just to get out from under the house," I said. "My old company isn't too popular right now, and nobody wants to hire anyone that worked for them. I don't know if I'll be employable."

"Uh, there's a second issue with the house. Maybe now is a good time to talk about that," Larry offered.

"A second issue? After the first issue, I don't know if I want to talk real estate anymore," I said.

"Yeah, a second issue. Have you ever heard of Chinese drywall?"

The conversation went downhill from there. Larry explained that basically, my real estate developer had become notorious for using crummy building products, after being successfully sued by several home purchasers who were sickened by conditions in their new homes. It turned out that the developer had used a product called Chinese drywall in many of its home-building projects. It is what it sounds like— drywall sourced from China. The drywall releases toxic gasses that can cause asthma, cough, and headaches, and damages metal pipes, wiring, and fixtures in homes. Larry let me know that any home built by this company would not have any chance at selling without substantial remediation, due to the builder's reputation. In essence, regardless of the "softened market", if I wanted to sell my home, I would have to gut and remodel the entire house.

"Wow, well, can I sue the developer, too?" I asked hopefully. *That would be great,* I thought. *I could win a bunch of money in court, punitive damages, and come out ahead. I could move and start over. Maybe in Costa Rica.*

"What kind of dickhead are you? Do you have any damages? Have you been sickened or suffered any physical ailments due to the condition of your home?" he asked.

"Well, no. I did notice that a lot of things broke right after the one-year home warranty period was up," I offered.

"Look, you can't go suing a developer without grounds or damages. You can only sue if you are harmed due to negligence or whatever. Ask your lawyer about it, but I don't think you can sue. And a couple of nail-pops after the first year are to be expected."

"Jesus Christ, so there's nothing I can do?"

"Look at you!" Larry snorted. "Aren't you jewish? Is that even a curse word for you? You aren't cursing, so much as you're hollering out to your dead second cousin three times removed or something. Hey, I'd love to chat all the live-long day, but I've got work to do. Your best bet is to hang tight in the house until you can pay for it or the bank throws you out, whichever comes first."

Chapter Two

No joke, people, my life was a disaster, and my house was the current headline. Okay, maybe that contractor didn't use Chinese drywall in my particular home, but he managed to construct it so that everything started falling apart nano-seconds after the home warranty expired.

On this particular morning, I woke up and stared at the ceiling. Unh. I didn't even want to get out of bed. I'd never felt this way before in my life. In high school I'm had sort of been aware that there were kids who were depressive, weirdos on Prozac, hating life, sleeping through morning classes. That was never me. I was pretty popular, and enjoyed going to school to hang out with friends and have fun. In college I might have missed a few morning classes if I was really hung over, sleeping in next to some hottie, but I count on that as pretty normal college life. Ok, one or two hotties. Ok, one hottie. Well, she was kind of hot. Regardless, when my job came along, it was always easy to pop up, get some exercise, have some coffee, hit the road. Life was always GOOD.

Today, though, it all hit me. I had nothing to wake up for.

I got up anyway. That's what you do, right? Get up,
take a shower, dress, live life. I took a leak and washed my
hands, then reached to turn off the bathroom sink. POP! The
right tap came off in my hand, and the water kept on running.
I stared at the sink. Water flowed. I tried to put the tap back
on, but it seemed as though some piece of metal had
completely snapped off, or maybe the screw was stripped, or
something. I don't know. I'm a little vague when it comes to
home repair, or anything terribly hands on. When I was in
junior high, I had taken woodshop, but hadn't done very well.
I was always jumpy because the teacher, a gruff older man,
kept wandering the shop hollering "Stop screwing around!
Someone's going to lose a finger if you don't stop screwing
around." None of us believed him, until the day my buddy Ron
was screwing around and ran half of a finger through a table
saw. The blood spurted as he turned white and passed out.

The teacher pulled the plug and hollered, "That's what you get for screwing around!" I jumped out of my reverie. The water kept running and running. I wasn't sure what to do.

At first I was tempted to just let it run. It ran and ran. Then I remembered how high my last water bill had been, and how I had no money. Not good. Maybe I could collect up the water and save it? I strolled to the kitchen, got a cereal bowl, and stuck it under the faucet. In just a few seconds it was full. I walked back to the kitchen and checked my cabinets—6 bowls, total. That wasn't going to get me very far. Vaguely, I remembered a lesson in grade school about turning off water while brushing teeth, and how many gallons of water flow per minute. Way more than I want to eat, drink, or bathe in, or save up in any way.

What about a plumber? If I was lucky, I could have a guy out at the house in a couple of hours, wasting a ton of water and costing a fortune for the rush job. I had no money to pay a plumber, no money at all. I stared at the sink. Water bubbled merrily out of the tap and slid down the drain. MONEY, down the drain.

I raced back to the kitchen. Several of the kitchen drawers had always been dedicated "junk" drawers, where the rubble and residue of life resided. Twisties, expired warranties for home appliances, leftover soy sauce packets from the Chinese restaurant, expired coupons, broken pencils, inkless pens, random screws. The bottom drawer of the kitchen cabinets held my few home improvement items. Duct tape, Bamboo skewers for the barbeque, various allen wrenches collected up over the years of self-assembling Ikea furniture, a hammer, and a small-zippered tool kit that I got to take care of my computer (back when I had a PC instead of a MacBook). I opened up the tool kit and stared. Screwdriver. Smaller screwdriver. Something that kind of looked like a screwdriver, but that had a socket on the end instead of a point. A small stick with a plunger on one end and three prongs on the other—looked like something my ex-wife would use to pull pickles out of a jar. Needle-nosed pliers. Regular pliers. Oh!

Regular pliers!

I grabbed the regular pliers and hurried back to the bathroom. Where the tap used to sit, there was just a metal bar poking up. I gripped it with the pliers and twisted. The water slowed. I readjusted my grip on the pliers and twisted further. The water turned off. I sagged with relief, and stared at the pliers. I started back to the kitchen with them, then hesitated, and left them on the bathroom counter. No telling when I'd be able to afford to have a plumber come out and properly fix the tap, but I still needed to use that bathroom.

So, my life sucked. I had no wife, I had no money, and I had no job. I'd totally given up on ever paying for my house or even selling the house. Given its sketchy condition and the soft condition of the housing market in general, my real estate agent made clear that in his professional opinion, I would have to *pay* someone to take it off my hands. Now that I knew that the house wasn't worth keeping, I certainly wouldn't waste any more money paying down my mortgage, but while I was waiting for the bank to foreclose, I still had to pay my other bills. After all, how could I ever find another job without a cell phone and internet access?

I decided to ask my dad for a loan. Not something that I ever thought I would do, or ever wanted to do. My relationship with my dad isn't the greatest. To label him a "sleazebag" would be putting it lightly. He drove my mother crazy, cheated on her, ignored me and my siblings, and then walked out on all of us when I was in junior high. The worst part is, he's such an easy-going guy that everyone still kind of likes him. What a jerk.

Dad lived in south Arlington. I jumped into my ride and drove out. It was a gorgeous day—bright blue sky, crisp air, and leaves just starting to turn. Fall was in the air. I punched on my radio and guffawed at the zany antics of my favorite morning show. Before I knew it, I drove up to Dad's house. I sat in the driveway for a minute, trying to gut up the courage to walk to the door. It swung open, and my dad's second wife, Ruth, poked her head out.

"Daaaa-aaanny! Is that YOU? Come on in, sweetheart!" she shrilled out.

Looking at Ruth is like looking at my mom, version 2.0. She's a little younger, and a little thinner, but otherwise, they are basically the same person. I couldn't figure out why my dad would bother to divorce my mother, only to go out, find a new version of her all over again, and remarry her (version 2.0).

"Hey, Ruth. How are you... Is dad around?" I asked, walking up the front walk.

"Oh, yeah, he's coming home soon. You going golfing with him this afternoon?" she asked, waving me in.

"Is he golfing today? I didn't know," I said, walking into the house.

My dad lives in a classic McMansion. Two years ago, he and Ruth bought a tumble-down Cape Cod on a postage-stamp lot, had it razed, and put up a house that takes up roughly 97% of the lot. The other houses along his street are 1950s era red brick bungalows, with modest driveways and carefully clipped lawns. This house leers two stories over the other cute neighborhood bungalows, with its pink and taupe brick façade, cut glass front door, and two-car garage, mocking up a faux high-quality exterior. The other three sides of the house were wrapped in cheap vinyl siding, like a tract home on steroids. Walking in the front door, the interior is just as ostentatious and nauseating as the exterior.

I have to say, the individual pieces in my dad's house are nice, but when it's all put together, the décor has the overwhelming sense that every item of furniture just fell of a truck somewhere. Maybe it's the plethora of leather upholstery on all of the overstuffed chairs, couches, and pillows. Perhaps it's the extensive electronics, with the enormous television, satellite feed, and surround sound. It could be the glass, golden gilt, and black iron that trim nearly everything else in the room. I don't know. Maybe my vision is tinted by the knowledge that my dad lists himself as "self-employed" on his tax return, and has never declared an annual income higher than $48K in his entire life.

On the couch was my half-brother, David. David is fourteen years old, and has been brought up with all of the fatherly love and attention that I never had. As a result, he is the most entitled and angry kid I've ever met. He hasn't yet discovered drugs or sex, and maybe that's the reason why he's openly hostile. Maybe if he ever figures out there's more to life, he'll just become sullen and secretive like all the other teenagers.

"Hey David," I said. "How's it going? How's school?"

"Go to hell," David said, not pulling his eyes off of the 52-inch flat screen on the wall. He furiously tapped a series of keys on his wireless keyboard, causing an eruption on the screen and wall-shaking explosive sounds to burst from the surround-sound speakers.

"Good talking, David," I said, walking into the kitchen.

My dad was sitting in the kitchen, drinking a cup of coffee and reading off his tablet device. Say what you will about the older generation and their reluctance to adopt new technology. My dad is living proof that the baby boomers can stay current, move with the times. He is and always has been an enthusiastic early adopter of new devices. When I was a kid, it was 8-tracks and Beta-max. Now, with my brother David, dad has an all-wireless house, including wireless keyboards, wireless mouse, and no wired phone lines. Dad also keeps a Maryland cell phone number, even though he lives in Virginia. He claims that the taxes are three or four dollars cheaper per month that way. I think he just likes to stay that half-step ahead of criminal prosecution by confusing federal investigators.

"Good morning, Dad," I greeting him. "Whatcha reading?"

"Hey, Danny! How are you? Up for some golf? I could use the company."

"Oh, Dad, thanks but—you know, watching my wallet. Sorry."

"Oh, yeah I read about your company. Wow, those sons-a-bitches. Cheating their way through life, huh? And getting paid multi-million dollar bonuses. What a scam!" Dad cackled his appreciation.

"Actually, I don't know whether there was any wrong-doing. There's an active SEC investigation, but so far no evidence that our executives broke any laws. It could be the by-product of overall economic conditions," I blathered on, a little blush rising in my cheeks. I sounded stupid, even to my own ears.

"Yeah, and I gotta bridge I'll sell ya. Danny, what, did they make you sign some kind of non-disclosure agreement? You sound like a fucking PR campaign."

This wasn't going well. I was supposed to be asking for money, and instead I was standing around parroting corporate bullshit and getting called on it by the King of Bullshit. I needed to move the conversation along, more in the direction of getting some money. I needed to pull the trigger. Oh, fuck. I couldn't do it.

When I was a teenager and he walked out on us, I hated my dad so much I thought that I'd never talk to him again. He left his family in the lurch. He was unreliable and emotionally unavailable. I swore that I'd never ask him for anything, and to this day I never had. I made my own way through school, taking out loans and working part-time. After college I did ok, getting a respectable job with real benefits and a W-2, marrying a nice girl who I treated well, and paying my taxes. I didn't gamble, I didn't cheat, I didn't whore around, and I paid all of my bills on time. Here I was—I'd lost it all, and I was desperate for money, but I'd be damned if I'd ask this man for a handout. I swallowed hard.

"Well... good to see you, Dad. You look good. I'd better be going, better let you get to your golf. See ya," I said, turning to the door.

"Hey. Hey Danny. Son," my dad said. I stopped, and stared at the kitchen door, my hand resting on the countertop. Another deep explosion from the living room caused the counter to vibrate under my hand. Wine glasses rattled and tinkled in the overhead hanging rack. "Son, don't let me hassle you. It's tough right now. I know. I've seen the tough times too."

Right, I thought. *You made the tough times.* My throat tightened up, and I swallowed again. A few drops pricked the corners of my eyes. *Oh God, don't let me cry in front of my dad,* I thought. "Look, I know you might need a little help right now. What do you say, you come work with me? You know, father and son. We'll make one hell of a scandal, get you some cash. Whattaya say?"

For a moment I considered it. Working with dad might give me short-term cash, but long-term it could result in a pile of legal trouble. Worse, it could result in my total loss of self-respect. Self-respect and a willingness to work hard in a legal endeavor were about all I had left. I turned and half-smiled at him. Put on the brave face. "Wow, Dad, that's really nice of you to offer, but I've got a couple of things in the works. You know, some job interviews lined up, some good opportunities. I'm going to be ok. Hey, you do look good. Get a little more sun on the golf course today, ok? I'll see you soon, Dad." And I walked out.

CHAPTER THREE

So, dad wasn't willing to offer something for nothing, and I too proud to ask. Since I valued earning money without the potential for indictment, I passed on the opportunity of going into business with him. Next stop on the gravy train—a trip to my brother.

My brother is one of the few lucky dot-com millionaires that actually made millions off of the Internet and cashed out before the crash. He's been hurrahed in several financial publications as a genius entrepreneur. I don't think he's actually that smart. He's just lucky. He sold one useless website for a bundle and hadn't put much cash into developing the next one when the market crashed. Thus, he kept most of his money, which he has since plowed into a disgustingly huge home and a series of predictable franchise businesses.

I pulled up to his mansion in Potomac and surveyed the house. It looked like the kind of place a professional athlete might buy if they just wanted to spend a bunch of money and knew nothing about real estate. The house was large and would have been attractive on the right piece of land, in the proper proportions to the plot. This house was set just a bit too far back from the street to give a pleasing proportion, and the landscaping was expensive and well-maintained, but ugly. I wondered if I would see my sister-in-law, Dina. For the duration of their marriage, Dina has had a full-time job, and that has been to spend Jason's money. Since he struck oil (figuratively) with his dot.com success, she's had to work overtime. It's not easy, but somehow she wakes up every day with a renewed vigor and fresh perspective on how to drain their joint checking account. I didn't see her Porsche in the driveway, so she was probably out at the spa, or the gym, or the salon, or the boutique, or the jewelry store, or the designers, or the interior decorators, or buying the original Magna Carta and getting it framed, or coordinating a party with hotel staff and caterers, or customizing a yacht. Or something. Anything other than stay home and spend time with her husband and kids. I got out of the car, walked up to the double-wide doors, and lifted the heavy metal knocker. The door pulled open under my hands, and two small bundles hurtled out past me, screeching all the way. I jumped back. *Spider monkeys!* I thought, *holy shit, don't those carry the Ebola Virus?* No, wait. It was just my two nephews.

"Stop!" screamed a young woman with a Spanish accent. Her long, dark hair was pulled loosely back into a ponytail. She was sensibly dressed in jeans and a sweatshirt, with a small set of gold hoops in her ears. "Oh, hi Mister Danny, good to see you," she said swiftly. She tore past me, grabbed the two kids, and hustled them back inside. "It's snack time now. Come eat your snack."

"Uh—hi. Is Jason home?" I asked, stepping inside to the marble-floored foyer. As expected, Dina was nowhere in sight. However, her newest acquisition unfortunately was. The polished table that usually graced the center of the foyer holding a large floral arrangement had been replaced by an angular metallic sculpture. It was painted orange, or perhaps was just heavily rusted and loomed sharply upwards into the vaulted ceiling. The walls surrounding the art were stuffed thickly with potted palms. The sculpture looked like something you wouldn't want to stand near without an up-to-date tetanus shot. I wondered when my last tetanus booster had been, grimaced, and inched my way around the artwork, towards the living room.

"Uncle Danny, Uncle Danny!" shrieked one of the kids. "Come have snack with us!" He danced up and grabbed me with sticky hands. "We're having juice and fruit rollups!" He yanked on me, causing me to lurch forward into a decorative palm. Our hands separated with an audible, sucking sound.

"Uh, thanks, but I'll pass," I mumbled. "Jason?" I called out.

"Danny, what's going on?" Jason asked, walking up behind me. He had the Wall Street Journal in his hands, open to the personal finance section.

"Oh, just coming by to say hey," I started. "What the hell is going on in your foyer?"

"Dina's latest," Jason said. "Her interior decorator got her sold on living art. Supposedly the palms are part of the piece. The artist calls it 'Deforestation'."

"Gotcha!" screamed one of the kids, popping out of the palm forest along the wall and squirting us with a squirt gun. The Journal was the first casualty of war. "You're dead! You're DEAD!"

"Hey!" yelled my brother, waving his arms. The Journal shredded in half. "Stop being chutzpah-dik!"

That's my brother. Yiddish when he wants to be. Chutzpah is that swaggering bravado that Jews love to hate, hate to love, the fresh-mouthed arrogance that every parent doesn't want their kids to have but sure as hell want their Saturday night comedian to have. It's the balls to do whatever you want and damn the consequences. When kids act out? That's chutzpah-dik. That's bad behavior.

"Chutzpah-dik! Chutzpah-dik!" shrieked one of the kids into the face of the other. "Chutzpah-dik!"

"Stop saying that!" screamed my brother. "Now you're chutzpah-dik too! Don't say that!"

"Zombie dick zombie dick!" screamed the first kid.

"Jeez," I said. "Where did he learn that kind of talk? He's only four."

"Ugh, I think they watched 'Land of the Lost,'" said my brother. "Will Ferrell. You know. I don't think they know that dick is a bad word. They just think zombie-dick is another Yiddish phrase."

"Holy shit, too funny. What else does he say?" I asked, intrigued. Sometimes kids are fun. Usually it's when they are torturing the hell out of my brother.

"Oh, all kinds of shit. Come on, take a load off," Jason invited, leading me into his living room. We plopped into huge, overstuffed leather couches. "Hey you!" my brother yelled towards the nanny. "Can't you take those kids outta here? We're talking here!"

"Jeez," I said, "can't you call her by name? That's a little rude, don't you think?"

"Well I would if I knew what her name was."

"Don't you know your own nanny's name? Haven't you had this nanny for three years now?"

"Look," he said. "First of all, she's not a nanny, she's an au pair. Second of all, they change every year. You can't keep 'em longer than a year. I haven't had her long at all. "

"WHAT? What are you talking about? What's the difference between an au pair and a nanny?"

"Your American nanny, do you know what she wants? She wants a thousand bucks a week, that's what she wants. She wants to live somewhere else, so she doesn't show up to work if she doesn't feel like it. And she wants federal holidays off, and sick leave, and two weeks vacation, and health insurance. And you gotta pay her Social Security taxes and stuff or the IRS comes after you."

"A thousand bucks a week? Are you serious?" Maybe I should become an American nanny. Then again, I hate kids, so maybe not.

"Yeah, I'm not kidding," he said. "And who the hell can afford that?" You can, you rich bastard, I thought. "Now on the other hand, your au pair lives in your house and costs a hundred ninety-five a week, and you don't gotta give her sick leave or health insurance, or pay any taxes on her, neither. The downside is they only stay a year. So why bother learning their names?"

Sometimes I think my brother is a total douche. At times like this, I know he is.

CHAPTER FOUR

Given that my brother is a total jerk, and too cheap to spend money on quality childcare for his own offspring, I figured that there was no use in asking him for any money. What the hell. I headed off to Harris Teeter to scope out my dinner. Wow, the Fresh Market looked pretty expensive—I needed to watch my cash flow until I started making some money. I wandered around the store for a while checking out the specials. In frozen foods, I found some microwave burritos on sale, 2 for $3. Not bad! I loaded up my basket with them. A week's worth of dinners for $15. *Good job, Danny!* I skipped the $15 bottle of wine, and instead spent $12 on a twelve-pack of Corona to go with the burritos. Not bad—I went from $25 per night for dinner and drinks to $25 for the week's worth of dinners. But saving a little money on groceries wasn't going to pay my other bills. I needed to get a job, and money in the meantime. I had heard from other unemployed friends that Virginia unemployment benefits were lower than the ones in

DC. Although I lived in Virginia, my job had been in DC, and I was entitled to apply for DC benefits. I decided to go down to the Washington, DC Department of Employment Services to apply for unemployment.

The DOES isn't in the nicest part of town, if you know what I mean. I'm a little uncomfortable driving my car into certain neighborhoods in Washington. After all, at this point, my car is almost the only thing I've got. I hadn't had any worries about crime in the past, but a few weeks ago, my neighbor's nanny got carjacked at a bar in the Adams Morgan neighborhood in northwest DC. If I got carjacked, I would have nothing. So, I decided to ride the Metro.

The Department of Employment Services is right off of Metro's Orange line. I rode on a grimy car, which smelled heavily of urine and mold. All of the seats were taken, so I had to stand, gripping a slightly moist pole. I need to get a flu shot, I mused to myself, noting the number of people coughing and sneezing with mouths uncovered. I would be lucky to get off this train without catching the plague. The trip seemed to last forever, with me gripping a pole where I could almost feel the bacteria squirming under my hands. Finally, I got off at the Minnesota Avenue Metro station in Northeast Washington DC. The DOES is a typical government building, with interior walls painted a well-intentioned, generic color that turned sickly and scuffed as soon as the paint roller hit the wall. Ultraviolet recessed lights buzzed overhead from behind aluminum grids. I sighed and approached a counter.

"Can I help you," barked an angry voice. I turned to see a large black woman walking up, dressed in a multicolor, polyester blouse, a long black skirt, and seriously heavy-looking clomping black shoes. She looked like the vice principal of my elementary school. I immediately felt intimidated and small, and vaguely as though I had been caught cheating at something. *It wasn't me*, I thought quickly, *whatever it was, I didn't do it!* She looked irritated, and I realized that I hadn't responded to her inquiry. I hesitated.

"Are you here seeking potential employees?" She snapped. I jumped.

"Uh, no. No I'm not," I stuttered. "Um, I'm here because I lost my job."

"Say what?" She sized me up and down. I was wearing a fairly typical outfit, pleated gray trousers, a pressed white shirt, and a tie. Then she fell into a bureaucratic trance, peeling out (without taking a breath), "Did you voluntarily separate from your last place of employment, or were you discharged for gross misconduct or misconduct other than gross misconduct?"

"Uh, no?"

"Are you participating in a labor dispute other than a lockout?"

"Um, no, but—"

"Are you unable to work, unavailable to work, or unauthorized to work if you are a non-US citizen?"

It was clear that I was going to have to just jump in and cut her off. She seemed capable of going on for days. "Look, I was just laid off. Most of the people at my company were laid off. It's just going out of business completely."

"So you are out of work due to a mass layoff? We have a special program for that. Services that we provide include training or retraining, classroom or vocational training, literacy and English for non-English speaking individuals, and preparation for the GED exam."

Wow. I was definitely out of my element, here. "Um, I don't think I need any of those services. I have a degree, and actually already speak English, haha," I offered weakly.

She gave me a dirty look, and said, "Well, what do you want then?"

"I actually just wanted to get unemployment assistance. I applied for a couple of jobs, but my prior employer has some legal trouble, and I think it's reflecting poorly on anyone that was employed there. I'm having a hard time getting an interview anywhere, and I'm starting to run short on money."

"Well, do you need to revise your resume? We have a resume workshop. Otherwise, you fill out the application and then start applying to jobs. We have many employers who have provided us with jobs that are immediate need, we can refer you to the employers and get you interviewed right away."

"I just told you, I've applied to jobs. Nobody wants me. I just need the money."

"You may not have considered these jobs, but we can get you visible to employers," she urged. "These are companies that we know are hiring. Let's take a look and see what we could send your way."

I hesitated. "What could there possibly be in my line of work? I really think that I applied to every job that's relevant to my field. It's not like I'm going to apply to service industry jobs. The professional positions that I'm qualified to fill are closed off to me, due to the taint of my prior employer."

"Look, you can tell me that all you want. How do I know? You could be some kind of knucklehead for all I know. We deny you benefits if you refuse to apply for, or accept, suitable work without good cause. There's jobs out there, you might think you're too good for them. We're not going to pay you taxpayer money just to sit around waiting for a management position to open up or something. If you want this money, you've got to be unemployed through no fault of your own, available to work, ready and willing to work, physically able to work, and you have to make at least two job contacts each week. You have to make a personal and continuing effort each week to get a job, using normal methods. Not just standing around with some sign saying 'will work for food.' And I'm going to make you prove that you are trying to get a job. You have to tell me where you're applying so that I can check and make sure. If they offer you an interview or a job, and you don't show up, I'm going to deny your benefits." She ended her tirade with a quick side dip of her head, hands on her hips. Her lips bunched up on one side of her face, and she stared me down like a bulldog.

Holy shit. Was she like this to everyone, or was this some special treatment, just for me? No way to know. "Two jobs a week? Okay. I can apply to two jobs a week."

"Good. Here's your first one. This employer just called today and wanted someone to start immediately. I'll call the manager and say that you'll be there tonight, 6 pm sharp."

She handed me a sheet of paper. Ugh, it was a big-box retailer. Great. Death by $10 per hour.

"Um, what about applying for unemployment, and doing my paperwork, and all of that?"

"Ha!" She laughed. It was a mean laugh, in my opinion. "You can do all that over the internet. Now get out of here."

Great. I had a job opportunity for a shitty job. If I didn't show up, I wouldn't get unemployment. If I did a bad job on purpose to get fired, I wouldn't get unemployment. And if I ever quit, I wouldn't get unemployment. Cripes, with my luck they'd love me, and I'd be employee of the month for the next 8 months. It looked like I was going to have to suck it up and work for Blow-Mart forever.

I wandered back to the orange line and rode it morosely back towards the center of the city. I've got to tell you, that visit to the Department of Employment Services really had me down. I looked up just as the train operator announced the train arrival at McPherson Square. That's the stop for the White House. Hmm. Might as well walk around and see the sights, until I had to report for my big job at six pm.

It was hard work getting out of the Metro station. McPherson Square touts itself as the stop for the White House, even though it's actually several blocks away from the First Family's home. It's also the stop in the business district for infamous K Street, professional home to many of Washington DCs lobbyists and law firms. It naturally gets a high volume of riders entering and exiting the station. At rush hour, the riders tend to be business people with laptop cases and android devices, rushing to their jobs. During the day, the riders are more likely to be tour groups. Tour groups are a special animal. They like to move in packs. They like to wear matching t-shirts or sweatshirts, or matching hats, in obnoxious colors that immediately identify the wearer as part of the herd. This matching concept makes it easier for the herd to control movement and prevent escapes (especially important for school groups). Tour groups are often led by very loud persons carrying umbrellas, with participants encouraged to "Follow the umbrella!" This collective behavior insures that the participants will get a very narrow, umbrella-centric view of our nation's capitol, but also goes a long way to keep participants from wandering into bad neighborhoods where they might be robbed, stabbed, shot or killed.

Since tour groups can't independently find their bearings anywhere, and rely solely upon the guidance of the umbrella leader, a traffic jam often occurs in Metro stations, to the great irritation of all DC locals (sadly defined as any person who has commuted through a particular Metro station often enough to know which way to exit without hesitating). When a tour group enters a Metro station, they cluster around the fare stations, anxiously trying to purchase and load SmartTrip cards for the group. They occupy every fare machine, in packs of people 10 to 20 deep. DC locals get very angry, as no fare machine is left available for the locals who know what they are doing. Worse, each tour participant, for this one and only act on the Metro, generally decides to go it alone and load their own card up, rather than giving cash to the tour leaders to efficiently load up cards (perhaps in advance!) for the group. Cards loaded, the tour groups swarm to and through the gates, and immediately stop after clearing the gates, blocking all other travelers from proceeding to the trains. The groups teeter on the edge of certainty, trying to decide which platform to go to. It is a veritable Schrödinger's cat—there is no way to tell where the group might go for the day!

Ultimately, I suppose the umbrella holder must flip a coin and make the call which way the group will go. They all proceed to the escalators, and fill up the escalators down to the platform, standing side by side. Classic tour group behavior! Standing side by side is in direct contravention of Metro-riding etiquette. Experienced Metro riders know that all riders should stand single file to the *right* on an escalator, permitting others to pass on the left. The hoard doesn't care. It could lose folks by standing single file! And this is America, dammit, we don't leave a man behind! Nobody is going to tell the hoard how ride an escalator!

Finally, the group gets to the platform, where they anxiously peer, waiting for a train to arrive. Inevitably, they are staring into the depths of the tunnel in the wrong direction, trying to spot the train lights. When the train arrives from the opposite direction, folks get startled and

antsy, occasionally letting out a scream or a laugh, then fall

into a worshipful, meditative trance as the train pulls up—

heads whipping back and forth again and again as each car

pulls by. The bell dings, the doors open, and the hoard

immediately tries to pile into the train. This effort is met with

mixed success, as riders are often trying to disembark from the

train. If just a few riders try to get off, they may have to fight

through the hoard, perhaps getting forcibly rolled back on to

the train. If another hoard is getting off the train, then the

battle of the hoards ensues, as both try to pass through the car

doors at the same time. Should a hoard successfully get

through the doors, then they all shuffle just onto the train and

go no further. The train operators routinely implore riders to

"move to the center of the cars!" but the hoard either does not

speak English or cannot comprehend that a person other than

the umbrella-holder may direct their movements while in DC.

If you are trapped in a car with a hoard, just give up on

fighting your way to the doors and exiting before they arrive at their destination. Give in--you are along for the ride.

The tour groups eventually must leave the train. Having blocked the doors for endless stops, with certain knowledge that if they don't stay right by the doors *they might miss their exit,* the tour will hear their arrival into their destination station announced by the train operator. More importantly, the umbrella holder will hear this announcement, and will direct the group to then exit the train. The group will shuffle out the doors—and STOP. Again, a tense moment, while the umbrella holders anxiously check maps and station exits, trying to decide which way to exit. After the call is made, the group will once again clog up the escalators riding side by side, impervious to the plight of any late commuters trying to hurry up the left side of the escalator. After exiting the turnstiles, the hoard coagulates one more time, waiting for each member to officially exit the Metro system before attempting to exit the tunnel and enter daylight.

Today, two different competing groups were scuffling to get onto the escalator at once, both groups led by vicious-looking umbrella holders determined to get their tours out and about as soon as possible. The Orange T-shirts appeared to be menacing the Purple Ball caps. I sighed, punched the button on the elevator intended to carry folks with wheelchairs and strollers, and rode up the urine-scented elevator to the daylight. I made my way down I Street, past the business district blocks and towards the White House.

There's a park across the street from the White House. It is rumored, in Washington DC urban lore, that when the first President Bush, that being George W.H. Bush, declared the War on Drugs, heroically shaking a ziplock baggie of crack cocaine stamped "EVIDENCE", said baggie was not truly from a DC evidence locker, but actually had been acquired via retail purchase by a White House staffer for the sole purpose of serving as a prop in the speech. Further rumor had it that the staffer had just stepped out to this park moments before the speech to close the transaction. Elements of this rumor ring true. After all, who could really believe that crack cocaine would stay undisturbed in a DC evidence locker?

Today, the park was filled with protesters. That's fairly common around here. People from Iowa, or New Mexico, or Oregon, will sit at home getting mad at the government for one thing or another, and then they'll gather together into angry groups and talk about whatever is making them mad. It might be the environment, or breast cancer. It might be lower math scores at their kids' school, or over-regulation of television, or prayer in the schools, or no prayers in the schools. It might be Israel, or Iran, or Tibet. It might be police brutality or police appreciation. It might be food purity, dislike of genetically-modified seeds, anger at corporate farming, or lack of meaningful benefits for part-time workers. It might be pollution from coal-mining and coal-burning plants, opposition to nuclear energy, anti-big Oil, or pro-solar energy. My favorite was the March for Literacy. One mom marched proudly, her hand-lettered sign reading, "We NEED better Scools." No kidding.

Regardless, whatever the cause, one thing leads to another, and then next thing you know, these folks are marching on Washington. They'll get a permit for a street march and off they go, marching downtown with their police-escorted protest parade, twelve or fifteen people walking abreast and chanting protest slogans, "Hey hey! Ho ho! Big Oil has got to go!" with police cruisers and motorcycles idling at 3 miles per hour front and rear, and traffic backed up for miles behind. The marches will end with a rally, protesting in front of the White House or dropping in on their Representatives in Congress to give them an earful. Usually, not knowing who's who, they end up chewing out some poor staffer, or even just the secretary in the Member's office. They protest with vigor, clearly proud of themselves, feeling like history in the making. It's a good thing that they don't know that Washington DC gets on average at least 5 protests a week. That knowledge might take away from their sense of accomplishment. I usually don't mind the protesters, as long as they don't bang on my car or scream at me.

Today's batch of protesters had some sound equipment, with a microphone and amplifier. Two black guys were standing next to each other, one with a microphone and one just nodding his head. Somebody was running a back-beat. Both guys looked like total criminals. One had close cut hair, was clean shaven, and wore a suit and tie. The other had a straggly beard, long hair picked up in an afro, relaxed jeans, sneakers, and a flannel shirt. *Dammit! Why has society stereotyped black men as criminals? And why have I internalized the fear? Can't I just look at them and see another man?* Shit. I have some inner work to do. I hung back a little, just in case they were packing heat, and listened to the black guy with the microphone rap about his anger over Wall Street and the government:

> "Fuck the system
> Fuck the system

Cronyism, separatism
Egoism, nepotism
All the fat cats
Watch each others' backs
We out workin' every day
They golf and drink and play
Fuck the system
Fuck the system
Shakin' hands behind closed doors
Our government is full of whores
Pimp out for fifty bucks, and you go to jail
Pimp out for fifty billion and your kid goes to Yale
If they be for the people then ya gotta wonder why
They got good health insurance while we watch our
babies die
Fuck the system..."

He trailed off but the back-beat kept going. He passed the

mike to the other guy, who started up again:

"...We're tired at home, yeah money is tight
While the rich get richer, hey you know that ain't right
Cause we got bills to pay and the kids are hungry
But Congress sits around, yeah they backin' the money
Man we're angry here, you just hear us talkin'
But the government says, son just keep on walkin'
Yeah get out of here now, don't trouble us none
Thought they were workin' for me, but they be havin'
fun
They think they playin' around but it won't be funny
Heads will roll someday soon if they keep keepin' the
money
Yeah the people are mad, yeah the people won't take it
We're fightin' for our lives, and you know we don't fake
it

Fuck the system, 'cause it's keepin' us down
And we're here to run the mother fuckers out of town.
Peace out."

The backbeat kept going, and he tossed the microphone to me. I stood there, frozen. I had gradually stepped closer and closer to him as he rapped. His words were moving. I identified with his anger and his rage, with his frustrations at the government and the sense that nothing was for me, it was all for the benefit of the elite rich. His was righteous anger, it was good, and I no longer felt the cynicism I had felt when I first came upon the protest. His words meant something to me. I felt my spirit rising, felt a warmth in my chest. I had found my people, people who I could identify with and who would be a support and touchstone through this troubling time. But why was he handing me the microphone?

"Hey, speak your words!" someone yelled. The backbeat stopped.

"Speak up or pass the mike!" another lady screamed.

"Oh," I said, startled. I was invited to join in their cause! Already I was one of them! "Oh!" The backbeat started again, and I began to bob my head, feeling the beat, trying to put together what I could say to express how bad it had all become. What a cathartic opportunity, I thought.

I cleared my throat, and began to speak:

"Um. Life is hard, I just lost my job.
My wife left me, and I'm, um, all alone.
Back in the day, I had it good
Working for insurance I was in a great mood.
Um, then my company collapsed
Yes, it all fell apart
Now I've applied for unemployment
I have to make a new start..."

Wow, who knew that I could rap! It was coming so easily. My words were just flowing out. My heart swelled. I wouldn't have to apply to that job, I could just rap with these protesters. Maybe they were connected to the rap underworld. If an agent heard me, this could be my big break. From failed insurance company to overnight, underground Jewish rap success! I would travel the country with my peeps and rap about injustice proffered by the motherfuckers. Whoever those

were.

>"My bathroom sink broke, and I'm using pliers
>To turn off the water, so my bill won't get higher
>I'm looking for a job, but my chances really stink
>I might have to work in retail, that's worse than my
broken sink…"

But then, I was interrupted by some hecklers.

"Hey, did you just say your company collapsed? Your

insurance company?" a big guy on the first row yelled. He was

in the middle of eating a hot dog. He had a deep tan, dark

shaggy hair, and wore a South Park T-shirt with a fresh

mustard stain on it. "SCREW YOU GUYS," read his T-shirt.

"I'M GOING HOME."

"You worked for that big insurance company that just

came down? You worked for Almost Too Big To Fail?" cried

someone back in the crowd.

"Uh, yeah—" I started.

The backbeat abruptly stopped.

"You don't belong here!" Big guy yelled. He threw down his half-eaten hot dog and started stomping towards me.

"What?" I anxiously scooted back, still gripping the microphone. Feedback abruptly screeched through the speakers. The first black guy smacked the microphone out of my hand, and I jumped away from him.

"You aren't one of us! You're part of the problem, not part of the solution!" screamed a woman holding a baby.

"I..." I scooted further back, and bumped into a tree.

The crowd started to surge. Collectively, the chant began to grow. "Part of the problem, not part of the solution! PART OF THE PROBLEM, NOT PART OF THE SOLUTION! PART OF THE PROBLEM, NOT PART OF THE SOLUTION!"

Someone roughly grabbed my shoulder. I jumped, but to my relief, it was a uniformed police officer. "Hey buddy," he offered, "You'd better get the hell out of here. Yesterday they beat the shit out of some unemployed lobbyist."

"What? Aren't you here to protect me?" A brief vision of a ride out of the chaos flashed through my mind. No doubt the riot squad would arrive soon, with tear gas and rubber bullets to subdue these maniacs.

"What?" He sneered. "Are you kidding me? The failure of your 'Almost Too Big To Fail' company made my retirement account drop by about 40% overnight. I'm not going to protect you. I'm the 99%. Now get the fuck out of here."

Incredible. I bolted, running flat out down the street for blocks until I was safely back in the business district, and then dashed into a Starbucks. I pretended to get in line, and hid behind a stack of Breakfast Blend, peering around the corner to see if anyone had followed me. Nobody had followed me. I drew several ragged breaths, trying to recover from the psychic horror of my close escape. The door jingled open again. I jumped, but it was just more coffee patrons, lining up behind me and chattering about the latest project in their office. I put my hand up on the shelf, wiping my brow with my other trembling hand. Unfortunately I tipped the stack. Bags of coffee beans went flying, knocking over elegantly constructed mountains of ceramic coffee cups and biscotti cookies. Two employees ran out from behind the counter to start cleaning up, and folks in the line yelled and berated me as they waited for lattes that weren't getting made. The manager came out and asked me to leave.

I agreed to go, but mentioned, "Hey, do you happen to be hiring right now…?" He stared at me blankly. "Right. I'll be going now."

Great. I am the one person in the entire universe that can't get a job at Starbucks. Blow-Mart, here I come.

CHAPTER FIVE

West of the I-395, on Route 7 in Virginia, you will find the Kingdom of the Big Box Stores. For miles on end, there are grocery stores, department stores, home good stores, clothing stores, electronics stores, camping gear stores, shoe stores, pet stores, furniture stores—you name it. I had been sent to work for a big box retailer that deals in almost every item for a home or family.

After riding Metro, getting grabbed by a mob and having to run from the protest, followed by a roll through the coffee beans, I was a little less than fresh. A quick shower and change of clothes put me in a slightly more positive mood. Not sure what to wear for retail, I put on a pair of pressed khaki slacks, a white button-down shirt, and comfortable loafers. I microwaved one of my frozen burritos to give me a little energy. Not bad. Pretty salty, though. I made a mental note to pick up some salsa next time I rocked the 'Teet, but otherwise, not too bad. I could make this work, I congratulated myself. Step one, get this job, and live on burritos for a while until a real job came along. I was really talking myself into the job opportunity. No problem, I thought. No sweat. This is a job getting offered to folks without a high school degree. This job is offered to people who can't speak English. You can do this. Just suck it up, go to work for 8 hours a day, get some cash, and start making your plans for the next steps. I wasn't sure what next steps those might be, but that could wait until after my shift.

Precisely at 6 p.m., I arrived at my potential employer. A middle-aged, pudgy white woman was the store manager on duty. "Hi, I'm Judy," she said. Her voice sounded like she smoked about a pack a day. Her smell confirmed it. Judy's once-blond hair had a solid two-inches of dark roots, and was pulled back into a ratty pony-tail. She was wearing a pair of rumpled khaki slacks, a white button-down shirt, and an orange smock branded with the retailer's name and logo. A plastic nametag with her name inscribed was pinned to the smock. "Let's get you started on the employee forms and get you started in the stock room."

"Um, don't you want to interview me first?" I asked. "Make sure I'm the right candidate for the job?"

"DOES sent you, right?" she asked.

"That's right."

"Well, then, you're hired. Let's get started, I have a lot of work to do and I need a smoke break."

"Hey, don't you even want to check my background? I might have a criminal record or something." I couldn't believe how low the standard was to get a job in this store. This couldn't be right.

"Oh, you're right. Do you have a criminal record?" Judy asked hopefully.

"No!"

"That's too bad," she lamented. "We get an extra tax credit if we hire ex-cons. Ok, after you fill out these papers, I'll show you where to start." Judy got me to put on an orange smock. A machine in the manager's office rapidly carved out my name on a plastic tag. I looked down at myself dubiously. I was Judy's man-twin.

I sat down at a computer terminal and punched my information into the standard employee application, and Judy waddled off to smoke a cigarette. Fifteen minutes later, we reconvened. Judy verified my social security card and I was officially hired. Judy led me back into the stock room. Through those magic doors marked "Employees Only" is a huge warehouse that sits behind the entire store. Shelves up to the ceiling were stuffed with crates of the merchandise to be unpacked and moved out to the showroom floor.

"Okay," Judy said, "I need you to get started. We need to get these boxes loaded up and shelved out front. It's a little early for that right now, but we needed you here for the paperwork and you filled it out a little faster than I expected. Pretty comfortable with the computer, aren't you? Good. For this job, you'll use a hand-held computer, this hand scanner. You just need to check the list on the scanner screen, pull each item off the shelf, scan it with your hand scanner, hit the button to show the item has moved from the warehouse to the floor, and then get it out there and get it shelved. You'll be doing this every night, from 10 to 6, so that the store is restocked every morning when shoppers come in. We're open 24 hours a day, so some folks might be shopping when you restock, but mostly it should be pretty quiet. You need to get all the inventory on the list restocked and shelved, with a nice appearance. Each shelf should be properly faced when you are done with it. You will also need to periodically check with the checkout clerks, to see if they have any inventory that needs reshelved. You get two fifteen minute breaks and a 30 minute lunch break. Here's your handscanner. Let me know if you have any questions." Judy coughed, swallowed back a little phlegm, and wandered out, leaving the phantasm of nicotine and tar trailing behind.

I got started. It took a while for me to find each item in the warehouse, and after I pulled the inventory, it took a while to find the right location to stock it in the mega-store. The merchandise was laid out in wide aisles that turned this way and that, creating a maze nearly impossible to navigate quickly or efficiently. I mused over the cleverness of the layout—it forced customers to pass by nearly every department, just to get out of the store. Recalling my prior job, I knew that nearly nothing in big business was arbitrary, and wondered how many hundreds or thousands of corporate hours had been logged designing the retail labyrinth. After shelving crates of navy blue towels, Flintstone vitamins, exercise DVDs, greeting cards, and floor mats for cars, it was time for my break. Judy bustled into the breakroom as I was pumping quarters into the soda machine.

"Hey Danny, how's it going?" She asked. "Have you met any of your coworkers yet?"

I hadn't. Judy took me to the front register and introduced me to Amaya, a short, round black woman with her hair covered by a scarf, and Roger, a portly Latino guy. Both Amaya and Roger were working as checkout clerks. After exchanging brief small talk, and receiving a shopping cart full of inventory to re-shelve, I finished my soda and went back to the warehouse. The next item on my list was "Bookcases (tall-unassembled)". I wandered around and found the boxes, and scrutinized them dubiously, then wandered back out to find Judy. She was outside on a bench at the front of the store, smoking again, and staring out into the dark night.

"Hey, Judy?" I called, trying not to get too close to the smoke, fearing that it might trigger my mild, intermittent asthma.

"Yeah, Danny, everything ok?" she wheezed through a blue cloud.

"I might need some help with the next item on my list. It's unassembled bookcases. The box is really long and heavy, and it says 'Team Assist' on it. Can someone help me lifting? It looks dangerous to do it alone. My doctor told me to be cautious with heavy lifting. It could throw my back out of alignment, or give me a hernia..."

"Danny, are you bullshitting me?" She demanded.

"What? No, I just want some help lifting this box. I don't want to hurt my back or anything."

"Hurt your back? Danny, are you making the case for workers comp? Are you some kind of malingerer? Complaining tonight, gonna wander in here tomorrow with a note from the chiropractor, huh?" I began to protest, offering my disbelief in chiropractors and homeopathy in general, but Judy brushed me aside. "Just looking to get injured and go out on disability, right? Wrong. That's it, buddy, you are off stockroom and onto the register. I don't need any phoney-baloney back injuries out of you." Judy flicked her cigarette butt off into the parking lot and stomped back into the store.

We went back up to the checkout registers. "Roger, you're back in the warehouse," Judy barked. "Princess here is on checkout. Amaya, you show him what to do. Don't let him lift anything heavy."

Roger gave me a dirty look as Judy stomped off, back towards the customer service desk. Roger logged out of his register, took my hand-scanner, and headed to the warehouse. Amaya came over and showed me how to get into my register.

"Look, punch in your employee ID here," she said. Her voice was low and soft, mellow and slow. "Key here when a customer comes up. Always greet the customers with a smile. Scan the barcode of each item that they have. If it's too big to come over the register belt, take this handscanner and scan it in their cart." She lifted the handscanner to demonstrate. "If there's a mistake, you void an item like this." She pressed a few buttons. "To total the transaction, press here." She pointed. "To void the whole transaction, here." Pointed again. "And I'm right here to help if you have a problem. Okay?" She smiled at me. Her front teeth were widely spaced, large and white. A heavy gold chain hung around her neck, dipping under her smock. Her dark brown eyes sparkled, and crinkled up in the corners.

Wow. I think this must be the first time all day that anyone had been nice to me at all, much less smiled at me. Emotions welled up. I love you, I thought. You treat me like a human. Wow. "Thanks," I garbled out, my voice a little choked. "I'll let you know if I need help."

Amaya turned back as a customer came to her line, and I spent a few minutes familiarizing myself with the register, ringing up bubblegum and tabloids, then voiding out the transactions. It seemed straightforward enough. Soon enough a customer came up to my line and began to throw merchandise onto the belt. Cat food. Cat food. Cat food. Cat food. Catnip. Cat litter box. Cat litter. Kitty collar. "Hi, how are you today?" I said. "New cat at home?" The man ignored me and continued dumping kitty toys, a cat bed, and cat brushes onto the counter. "Want any flea bath to go with that?" I joked. He froze, and then punched a bunch of numbers into his cellphone. "Wow, would it be too much to ask to give a guy a little eye contact?" I mumbled to myself, scanning in his items one at a time. I totaled up the purchases. "Two hundred twelve and seventy three cents," I said. Wow, not too bad! He swiped his credit card, signed the digital display, and I punched the button to finalize the transaction. "Thank you, Mr. Anderson. You saved fourteen dollars and twenty-two cents," I announced, handing him the receipt. My first sale! I was proud. He pulled the receipt flat and scanned it over closely, then threw his bags into his shopping cart and marched straight off to the customer service desk. What?!

I saw him animatedly speaking with Judy, pointing first to his bags, then to his receipt, and then back at me. She looked up at me, then looked at him and nodded, said something, and then shook her head. They both stared at me, and then shook their heads. She said something again, punched a few keys on her keyboard, swiped his credit card, handed him his card and a receipt, and then he laughed and left the store.

Oh no. "Amaya, what did I do?" I asked quietly.

"Hmm? Oh, honey, that customer comes in all the time. I think he's got social problems. He's always buying stuff for cats. He gets really mad if you say anything. He also counts the cans of cat food and stuff and then calculates what his total is on his cell phone calculator. He asks for money back if you've rung up too many cans, but if you've undercharged him, he just walks out the door. Don't worry about a thing."

Cripes. I overcharged him maybe 47 cents on cat food, and he's complaining to my manager. "Wow, that's not a material amount," I mumbled to myself. "It's really just lost in the rounding. Why's he so mad." I guess I just need to go slower, I mused to myself. *47 cents isn't much to me, but it's important to the customer.* I needed to get this right.

When the next customer came along, I was more careful. A heavyset woman in Levis and a leather jacket began unloading a very full cart. Her salt-and-pepper hair was cut butch short and she wore a lot of silver and turquoise jewelry—dangling earrings, oblong rings, big chunky necklace. It took forever for her to unload her cart, so I went ahead and started ringing her up. Paper towels. Toilet paper. "Hi," I smiled at her. "How are you doing tonight?"

"Kind of in a hurry," she said. I kept ringing the stuff up, scanning each item carefully. Trash bags. Tampons. *No comment*, I thought. Mouthwash. Toothbrush. "That's three toothbrushes?" I asked. "Whoops, I put in four. I'll void one." I pressed a button, but instead of voiding just one toothbrush, it voided the whole transaction. "Oh no," I said.

"What?" the woman asked. "What happened?"

"I'm sorry," I said. "I voided your whole transaction. I'm going to have to re-scan all of your items."

She sighed a deep, heavy sigh, and I started to scan her items in again. Naturally, after I completed her transaction, she rolled her cart straight off to the customer service desk, where she began to yell and wave her arms at Judy. I stared straight at the floor, my face bright red.

Come on, Danny, I said to myself. *You can't keep this up. Get it right. You have a master's degree, for God's sake. You used to prepare quarterly reports for a huge insurance conglomerate. You can ring in a few sales. Get it together.*

A friendly-looking couple rolled their cart up to my register and began to unload their items onto the belt. "Hi!" I said. "How are you today?"

"Great!" They both replied enthusiastically. My spirits rose. Here were some nice customers! I'll take good care of them and send them on their way, I thought. I carefully rang in each of their items, one at a time, taking a moment between each item to check the screen and make sure that the item was properly registered. They stood waiting while I rang up item after item. The woman's cell phone rang. She answered it.

"Hello?" She said. "Uh huh. Uh huh. Yeah. I'll be there soon, maybe. I don't know. I've been in line forever while the world's slowest checkout clerk rings up our stuff. I might die here in line, I don't know. Ok, hope to see you soon. If I don't make it, tell my kids I love them. Ok, bye." I didn't even try to look her in the face as I handed her the receipt, and watched the two of them roll on up to the customer service desk.

"Oh honey," drawled Amaya, "You ain't having no luck tonight. Oh sugar. What are we gonna do with you?"

She calmly rang up her customer without issue, smiled and said goodbye, and then turned to me. "Look," she said, "You can't let Mr. Anderson mess you up. He's just a crazy. These customers don't really care if you charge them for two toothbrushes or three. They just want to get out of here two minutes faster. You're the last person between them and the door, and out the door is where they want to be. Just ring their stuff up. Most of them don't look at their receipts, and don't notice that it's two dollars over or whatever. Look, a lot of customers are in such a hurry that they even leave some of their bags here. We don't chase them down or anything. We hold it to the end of the day, and then restock the stuff back to the shelves. The store sells it all over again. Just ring the next customer up normal, and the next one after that. You'll be alright. And if you do it wrong, let me help you void it out so you don't have to ring it all up again."

Well, that was optimistic. When the next customer came along, I began to shake. The man looked at me dubiously. I pushed a button, and my register locked. "Amaya," I called out. "I don't know what it's doing. Help."

Amaya turned away from her register, where she had been making change for the customer. "Oh sweetie, you do this." I stared at her hands as she leaned over and pushed several buttons. "Now go ahead."

I finished ringing up the transaction, and watched morosely as, once again, my customer headed off to Judy. "That's it, I'm cooked," I said to myself.

"What, honey?" Amaya asked.

Judy headed over to me. "Look," she said. "I don't know what to say, but the customers hate you. I can't keep you here, you're awful."

"Please don't fire me," I said. "If I'm fired for misconduct, I don't qualify for unemployment. I'm sorry, I'll do anything. Please let me stay on."

"I'm sorry, I just can't do that. I'm not letting you go for misconduct, though. You just aren't the right fit. I can let DOES know that we need someone with more practical retail experience. You seem overqualified for this job anyway. Ask them if they can get you something more suitable for your skillset."

And that was it. Blow-Mart let me go.

CHAPTER SIX

I was sitting on Judy's bench in front of the store, staring out into the night and wondering where my life went wrong. *Maybe I should take up smoking*, I thought, when a hand touched my shoulder. I jumped.

"Relax, honey," drawled Amaya. She sat down next to me.

"Are you on break?" I asked.

"Oh, no, sugar, I just got let go."

"WHAT? But you were doing great! What happened?"

"I guess when I was helping you, someone leaned over and grabbed some credit card receipts out of my till. That's mandatory termination, if someone steals because the till is unattended."

"You're kidding! Did they get any cash?" I asked.

"No, just the receipts. That opens the store up to more liability than just cash."

"Why? My credit card receipts only show the last four digits of my card number. Who cares? Can't the store just pull the transactions up on the computer?" I asked.

"Well, the receipts that get printed up for the till have the full number and expiration date. Someone could use that information to charge up a lot on the cards. If the store is negligent, and the credit card companies have to deal with fraudulent transactions, they will come after the store."

"I'm so sorry," I mumbled, shaking my head. My lips felt numb. I couldn't believe it. My incompetence had caused a perfectly nice woman to lose her livelihood. "I don't know what to say. I don't know how I can make this up to you. Amaya, I'm sorry."

"Don't be sorry," she said. "It's ok. I always have a backup plan. If I can't find another job, I'll just go work at my cousin's 7-11 down the street. No worries."

I gave Amaya my cell phone number and made her promise to call if she had any trouble finding a job. I wasn't really sure what I would actually do if she called, but I felt like she should at least have the opportunity to hunt me down and run me over or something. God, what an asshole I am.

Amaya thanked me, and patted my shoulder one more time. Then she told me, "Honey, you worry too much. God loves you. It's really going to be okay." And then she walked off into the dark parking lot, and was gone.

I went home and tried to go to bed. I tossed around for a while, feeling guilty, trying to wind down from my crappy day. I popped back up, chugged a beer, watched some re-runs on TBS, and finally drifted off to sleep. When I woke up, I wandered into the kitchen to microwave a burrito. This cooking stuff was a new adventure for me. When Lacey was around, she cooked most of our organic meals from scratch, and we ate out on occasion. After she left, my meals were prepared by Clyde's, and then by the grocery store chicken-roaster. Here I was venturing into the new and exciting world of cuisine! I pulled the burrito out of the freezer, threw it onto a plate, and put it in the microwave. I punched in 2 minutes and hit the "Start" button. The plate spun around and around for a little over a minute, and then the microwave abruptly died. The microwave had lost power.

I pulled the door open and closed it again. Lights still out. Hmm. The microwave was built into the cabinetry above the range, and I wasn't sure how to check the power source. No power lines were visible. I went downstairs to the check the breaker box in the basement. Maybe I had somehow tripped a switch? The box had 40 switches lined up in two columns, and the contractor that built our house had kindly failed to label any of the white spaces next to the switches. Shit.

So this was my morning project. I turned on all the

lights in the house, and started flipping breaker switches.

Might as well, I had nothing else to do with my day. As I

flipped each breaker switch off, I ran around the house to find

out what set of lights and outlets went out, then ran back to

the basement to label the switch. After an hour and a half, I

had all of the switches labeled, and each switch was flipped

back on. I went upstairs to check out the microwave. Still

dead, and I by now I was starving. I pulled out the burrito. It

seemed to be room temperature, so I took a bite. A little cold.

The next bite was crunchy—the burrito had a solid chunk of

ice, a half-inch thick core of frozen beans and cheese. I gnawed

around the frozen beans as best I could, then threw the rest

away in the trash can. I looked in the freezer at the rest of my

stash of burritos, and pulled one out to see if there was any

other way to prepare it.

"Microwave on HIGH for 2 minutes," I read, "or bake in

425° oven for 35 minutes." I stared at the oven. It was a

mysterious creature, a double-oven built into the wall with a complex set of buttons programming both ovens at the top. I stared at the buttons, and pushed BAKE. Nothing happened. I pushed SETTINGS. Nothing. TEMPERATURE. The double oven obdurately blinked the current time at me. I punched the double arrow up. Nothing. Cripes. I turned my attention to the microwave, still dark and blank. God, I wish Lacey would take my calls. She could tell me how to work the oven, or at least where to find the owner's manual. I looked up to the ceiling, almost as though to implore God for help, and noticed that there was a cabinet above the microwave, so I pushed a bar stool over and climbed up to look into it. As I swung the cabinet door opened, I saw that the cabinet was mostly filled with the ventilation shaft for the range vent. It also had an outlet, with a plug already plugged in. Eureka! I unplugged the plug, looked at it, and then plugged it back in. I checked the microwave—still dark. Hmm. The outlet had a trip switch built into it. Maybe just the outlet was tripped. I pushed the button, unplugged and plugged in the microwave. Still dark. Damn.

Oh well. I drank a beer and thought about how shitty my life was, then noticed a funny smell. I wandered into the dining room and noticed that the light switch for the dining chandelier was smoking. Oh, hell! I ran downstairs and frantically scanned the newly labeled breaker switches until I found the one for dining room. I flipped it off, then ran up to check the dining light switch. The dining room chandelier was dark, and the switch wasn't smoking any more. This called for another beer. I opened up another Corona, and slouched at the breakfast bar to drink it. Obviously my house had some wiring problems, but I couldn't afford an electrician to fix the wiring, any more than I could afford a plumber to fix my bathroom sink. The microwave powered back on again. WTF.

The next morning, there I was. Back at DOES, but hung over this time. I had drank my whole week's worth of beer in one day. I had no choice—the microwave kept blinking out if I ran it for more than one minute at a time, and I couldn't get the oven to work, no matter what I did. My kitchen appliances were possessed, leaving the beer as my only source of sustenance. Hopefully the morning's shower and a good round of mouthwash had helped to make me a little less beery. I walked through the doors, and ran into the same career counselor almost right away.

"Oh, hi, um—I didn't catch your name last time," I offered.

She gave me a cold look up and down. "Pam," she stated. "Pamela Washington."

"Oh, hey, Pame—uh, Ms. Washington, great to meet you," I gushed, grabbing her hand and pumping it up and down. "Daniel Rosenberg. Really good to meet you. I went down to the employer that you referred me to, and gave it a try. I just wanted to touch base with you and debrief on the wins and losses of that particular transaction." I belched a little into my other hand, and tried not to sweat.

Pam snorted. "Are you for real?" She looked at me. "You are for real. You really did go down there. Wow. Mr. Rosenberg, good for you. You made contact and tried to get a job. Let's sit down, ok? Let's go to my office."

We walked down the hallway, ultraviolet lights buzzing overhead. "Those irritate my brain cloud," I mumbled.

Pam turned towards me. "Say what?" she asked. "Do you have a medical disability?"

"Oh, no. It's from 'Joe Versus the Volcano'—the movie. You know, Joe works under these kinds of lights, and feels awful, so the doctor tells him he has a brain cloud," I explained, waving my hand over my head to demonstrate "brain cloud". "You know, the movie," I finished lamely.

"Guess I missed that one," she said.

"Yeah, you'd have to see to believe it," I mumbled.

We sat down in her office. Grim industrial walls. More ultraviolet lights buzzed overhead, casting a sick glow over the room. Pam had cheap government office furniture. The fake wood veneer on the side of her desk was peeling off the side of the particle board slab, and held in place with an oversized binder clip. My chair was injection molded plastic on chrome legs, uncomfortable. Pam had a montage of pictures on the wall, happy looking family photos with tons of kids, moms, dads. "Nice pictures," I offered. "Are those your family?" I figured they were brothers and sisters, nieces and nephews. But wait—on closer look, some of the pictures were clearly white families, and some Asian, and Hispanic. *Strange*, I thought.

"Yes, these are my family. Every so often, when I've helped someone find permanent employment, they send me in a holiday card. Sometimes there's a family picture in it. I always put them up on this wall. It helps to remind me, this is why I come to work every day—to help people get on their feet, make the money, afford to take good care of their families. Help them get to a place where they can go down to Picture

People and spend too much money on a little family portrait. Yes, it's my family."

"So, Mr. Rosenberg," she continued, "Wins and losses. Tell me how the job went."

"Well, it didn't go so well," I said candidly. "I did what you said, showed up, and gave it a try—and they gave me a try, too. So we all tried. They put me in the ware house to pick out stuff and restock, but I didn't know how to lift right or something. I was afraid of hurting my back, and they were afraid I would hurt myself. Then I was put on register, but the customers all complained that I was too slow, and no good. The manager said they are looking for someone with more practical retail experience, and said to ask you if there is a job that aligns better with my existing skillset."

Pamela gave me an appraising look. "Okay," she said. "Last time you were here, you said that you didn't think you needed our resume workshop. Did you bring a copy of your resume?"

"Yes, I have it right here," I said, pulling a flash drive out of my pocket. Pamela took it and examined it critically. She plugged it into her computer and asked, "Which file is it? The only file on here marked 'Resume' is an excel spreadsheet."

"Yeah, that's it," I said.

"What?" Pamela looked at me incredulously. She punched a few keys and opened the file. "You put your resume into an excel spreadsheet? Who does that?"

"We used excel for all of our reports and stuff at my old job. It's really easy to format," I offered.

"Danny, it's called Word. Microsoft Word. You know, for documents that have words in them. Did you give this resume to any prospective employers in file format?"

"Yes, most of them got it electronically."

"And you never wondered why you didn't get picked up for a job?" Pam snorted. She stared at the screen for a few minutes. I guess she eventually got over the file format and got into the substance of my pathetic resume. "You worked for Almost Too Big To Fail?" she asked. "No wonder you can't get a job in your old industry. Your old company poisoned the well."

"Thanks."

"No problem. Look, let's look at your qualifications other than your previous employer. You had an internship in school. You have a Masters' in business. Hmm. Your hobbies listed include wine-tasting and cooking foreign cuisine. Maybe you can wait tables. You also state that you like skeet shooting. Do you own a gun?"

"Yes, I have a shotgun and a handgun."

"Ok, so you own a firearm. That's part of your skill set."

"What? What kind of job can you get with a gun?"

"Well, depending on what type of permit you have, you might be able to work security or similar. Let's not pin you down to any particular profile yet, though, let's explore all of your strengths and see where it leads us."

Fair enough. I liked that she was thinking outside the box. Brainstorming. "Sure," I enthused, "Let's put that one in the parking lot." She gave me a quizzical look. It was clear that DOES was NOT sending its employees to corporate trainings where everyone drinks the buzzword Kool-Aid.

"Alright, memberships. You are a member of several industry groups, as well as the BMW Car Club of America? Do you have a BMW?" she asked.

"Yes, I do, a 535i," I said.

"Leased or owned?"

"Oh no, it's mine. Bought and paid for. Last payment was 10 months ago," I said proudly. "Leasing a car never made financial sense to me. See, I ran a couple of spreadsheets with different assumptions, and the conclusions remained that if I wanted to drive a car for more than the first two years, the better outcome lay in…"

"Uh huh," interrupted Pam. She gave me a sharp look. "Do you know the difference between a BMW and a porcupine?"

"Is this a mock interview question?" I asked nervously.

"Porcupines have pricks on the outside!" she crowed, and then broke into peals of laughter. Oh God. She hated me. I sat stiffly and nervously while she wound down her laughter and wiped the tears from the corners of her eyes. She chuckled to herself a few more times, and slapped the desk a time or two. "Pricks on the outside!" she whispered, "Hah!" She took a couple of deep breaths, and then looked at my resume and back at me.

"Car ownership is part of your skill set," she said. "How is your driving record? Clean?"

"Sure," I replied. "No tickets, no points, nothing. Where does my car get me?"

"Oh, you never know. There could be various jobs where driving would be part of the duties. Deliveries. Courier opportunities. Is your driver's license personal or commercial?"

"Um, personal. Just a regular license."

"Can you drive a motorcycle?" she asked.

"No, sorry. No bikes. They aren't very safe."

"That's ok, you don't worry about that. Let's see, what else. Hobbies. Spanish language. You speak Spanish? There could be some possibilities there, based on your level of competency. And—you like to go boating. Ok. Let's do this." She clicked into her computer for a few minutes, clickety clack, and finally hit "Print."

I sat up straight and waited to hear her words of wisdom. I sincerely hoped she would have a golden opportunity for me, something that would make the past few days seem less hellish and more like a funny memory – something that would dwarf the negative with its awesomeness and put me back on the path to financial solvency.

"Here you go. Beauties," she said, handing me a warm sheet off the printer.

"Pardon me? A beautiful job?"

"No, Beauties. It's a club. They need a security guard. They asked for former police officers or off-duty military to be referred, or other applicants that are comfortable around firearms. It's here in Northeast."

"Oh." I sat back. I didn't know that it was okay to have a firearm in the District, but who knows. "I guess I'll give it a shot. What kind of club is it?"

Boy, did I ever find out. Beauties was a gentleman's club, and Beauties employed dancers. I had been to a couple of strip clubs before—once for my bachelor's party, and once in Las Vegas. I remembered the girls at those clubs looking soft, limber, and pretty. The looks ranged from sweet girl next door to hard-edged, S&M hotness. These girls were just a little different. I don't know if you would call these girls classic beauties—I mean, they had a certain look to them that told me not to touch if I was interested in maintaining my health. They looked a little dirty, tall, strong. I wondered if it would be possible to spray them down with some Lysol, and then touch. No, even with Lysol, I don't think I'd want to touch.

The manager at Beauties introduced himself. "Name's Al, Al Frasier," he said, pumping my hand up and down. Al's hands were soft from lotion, and he reeked of cologne. He was a mid-height, African-American gentleman, dressed in pressed slacks, a soft blue dress shirt with French cuffs threaded with gold cufflinks, and suspenders. I looked down at myself. In comparison, I was dressed in jeans, a T-shirt, and a hoodie, with banged-up sneakers on my feet. I suddenly felt underdressed. "Come on in here, Danny. So. You look fit. Maybe a little short. That's ok. So, you're comfortable around crowds? You're ok with the dancers? Ok to look, but don't get distracted, you're on the job and you gotta watch out. You're comfortable around firearms?"

I assured him that I was fine with everything. "Listen, Al, I was wondering. I didn't know that it was legal to carry firearms in the District. I guess they give you permits for the club?" He gave me a look. "So, will I need to carry a gun?"

Al laughed as he walked me past the bar, taking a moment to check his look in the mirror and smooth his 'do. "No, son. You need to be comfortable in case a customer has a gun. Look, some of these guys come in here, they might be a little nervous about protection. They be from some rough neighborhoods, they want to feel a little safer while they have some entertainment. So they carry a piece. That's how they roll. But if two guys carry in a piece at the same time, and they're from different blocks, it might get noisy. That's when I need a guy who's comfortable around firearms. You can't just run off. Someone's gotta hustle the dancers out of here and call the cops. That's where you come in. Ninety-nine percent of the time you're just working the line. That one percent of the time, we're relying on you to keep us all together, make sure we get out safe and the cops show up."

"Are you shitting me?" I asked. "I'm supposed to stand here during a shootout and call the cops? The DC cops. The ones who take 45 minutes to show up. They'll show up 10 minutes after my last pint of blood has leaked out, just in time to see your customers throw my looted body into the dumpster and drive off in my car."

"Now son, don't get all worked up. It's bad for your blood pressure. That's an urban legend, too. The DC cops don't take 45 minutes to show up. That only happened once or twice. DC has fine police, fine, fine police. Now, I'm offering you this position, so think long and hard before you turn me down. I know that DOES sent you, and if you say no, you won't get your unemployment check." Al gave me a long, appraising look, and ended with a nod.

Aw, hell. He had me right over the barrel. He didn't even bother whispering something sweet in my ear before he shafted me. I had to take the job, and make the best of it.

I let out a long sigh. "How much does it pay?"

"This here is a salaried position, so you get paid per night, not per hour. It's $50 per night. Club is open from 6 pm to 2 am."

I did the mental math. *Let my people go!* I thought. "That's only $6 per hour! That's not even legal!"

"Don't get fussy at me. You get your salary, and then there's tips. The dancers aren't the only ones making tips here. You get gratuities, you know what I'm saying, based on how you control the line and the door. You've got to exercise some discretion about who you let in. We get some major players in here, sometimes athletes and musicians, some politicians, business people too, and some of them are very grateful if you forget their faces. Other people in the line are very grateful just to get in. They like to express that gratitude in the financial sense. The last security guy we had was pulling in a few Gs a week." I looked at Al again, noting the gold cufflinks, the diamond pinky ring, a sapphire-inlaid tie clip.

I wondered what had happened to the last security guy, but I was too afraid to ask. Some tales are best left untold.

"Look," said Al, "The main part of your job is to make sure that we don't violate fire code. We've got the bartenders in here, the DJ, the dancers, you, and me—usually around 15 to 20 staff altogether. By our square footage and exits, we can only have 235 people in here at once. Your job is to make sure we have enough people in here that it looks full, enough people in the line that it looks popular, and enough capacity to handle the real players when they show up for some fun. You know? I'll help you out at first, let you know who's who, so you don't have anyone important getting impatient in the line when they should already be in the club." He set a couple of "Reserved" signs on tables closest to the stage. "We're expecting a couple of real players tonight, I'll clue you in when they get here."

The night began. Dancers limbered up. I stood at the door. A line began to form. It was up to me to filter who came in and who didn't. At first I just let folks in. The first 50 or so were no-brainers. The club was totally empty, and they were the ones desperate enough to show up right when it opened. They sailed straight for the bar and ordered drinks, changed twenties for singles, and then spread out to the closest, unreserved tables they could find near the stage.

After that, I got a little more selective. I put a belt across the door and let a line form. I went back and looked at it after a few minutes, selecting the better-groomed and more attractive people waiting, and let them in. Admittedly, among this crowd, the term "more attractive" meant that they had diamonds on their gold teeth, and "better-groomed" indicated that the tattoo-artist ran spell check before inking them up. As Al mentioned, a few of the less-attractive line riders reached out to shake my hand, palming cash. I let in a couple of hundreds and several fifties. I let in a few marginally attractive twenties. I pushed back the fives and tens. What, did they think I was running a charity here? Slowly, I filled the club with people that I would typically run away from in a dark alley. When occupancy reached about two hundred, I put the belt back across the door and stood by. The line grew longer and longer.

At about 11:30, Al ran up to me. "They're coming, they're coming," he hissed. "These guys are major players. This is great, it's huge for the club. A couple of them are from here, and they brought some guys from out of town."

A couple of stretch, Humvee limos pulled up in front of the club. Out of them ambled the biggest men that I had ever seen in my life. My jaw dropped. I had seen some of these guys on Monday Night Football! Al was right, these were real players. I couldn't believe it. My hands got sweaty. What should I do? Should I ask for an autograph? Should I ask for a picture? This was unbelievably incredible. Should I profess my man love for them?

"Stay cool," muttered Al. "Stay cool. Just be a professional. Treat them with respect."

The players walked up and blew right past the line. Clearly they knew that there was no expectation for them to wait for admittance. These guys were kings. I opened the rope and stood aside to let them in. As they walked past, a couple of them nodded at me. I grew light-headed. Major pro athletes, acknowledging my existence! A smaller guy trailed after them, who had followed out of the second Humvee, shaking my hand and palming me a wad. This guy must be the flunky, greasing the wheels and taking care of people for the players. After they made their way into the club, I discreetly checked the wad in my hand. Five hundred bucks! No wonder men put themselves in the way of danger to work this job. I had cleared almost a thousand bucks on the night, not counting the piddly fifty bucks that Al was paying me.

Al was schmoozing the guys. He ushered them up to the "Reserved" tables, right in front of the dancers. I got another look at the girl on the stage and shook my head. Her face was angular, with a square chin and flat nose. Really not pretty. I wondered what these guys saw in the dancers. Al hustled up some bottle service for the tables, and the DJ started a new song. Two dancers began performing at once, dressed in bondage clothes, chained to each other by the neck. They waggled pierced tongues at each other, and took turns lightly spanking. The dancers moved on to complicated spins around one of the stage poles, using the neck chain to great effect. The players drank and kicked their feet up onto the table. A couple of dancers wandered up and settled into laps, smiling and whispering. I stepped back to check the line and the door. A couple of guys in over-sized jerseys, towards the front of the line, were scuffling. One was in a Redskins jersey, and one was in a Dallas Cowboys jersey. What a fucking pain. In the NFC East, the Washington Redskins and Dallas Cowboys maintain a notorious rivalry. The Redskins are the local team, and everyone here knows it. But this city is full of contrary dipshits that crave attention and take it anyway they can get it. Said dipshits typically express their neediness by putting on a Cowboys jersey and agitating a crowd.

"Hey, cut it out," I bellowed. "Cut that shit out. Don't make me throw you out of here." They gave me sullen looks and stopped pushing. The player's flunky ran up and pushed past me, grabbing the guy in the Cowboys jersey.

"Hey man, he's with us," he said softly to me. He pulled the guy into the club.

"Okay," I said, letting him pass. Far be it for me to stop the guy who greases the wheels. As far as I was concerned, he could let in a few more buddies. The club had capacity, and he was my new best friend. He could come every night, as far as I was concerned. The two stepped back up to the front tables, and I resumed my place at the door. The other scuffler, the Redskins jersey, spit a huge wad next to my shoe. I jerked my head up.

"Yeah, that's right, fuck you," he said. "And you look just like that bitch, Hillary Clinton." He spat again and walked off.

I was stunned. What was that supposed to mean? I'm not blond. I'm not a woman. I don't have baggy eyes, or a thick waist. No cankles. Hillary Clinton? I'm not even weighed down by matters of state. Who knows. That guy was probably a junky, and out of his mind. He was angry that I wasn't letting him into the club. Just let it go, I mentored myself. I checked back into the club.

The flunky and his needy Cowboys friend were back up at the tables with the players. Everyone was laughing and joking. One of the players pulled out a roll, and began passing bills around to the dancers, the flunky, and the flunky's friend. The player pulled off a bill for himself and rolled it up tight, and then leaned down over the table and snorted up a line, popping back up a few seconds later. Oh no. I made sure the rope was secure in front of the line, closed the door tightly, and stepped inside.

My eyes frantically scanned the room. Al, Al, Al. Where the hell was he? I finally spotted Al, over by the DJ. I hurried up. "Al, Al, hey man, hey," I breathed into his ear.

"Hell, no! Stop slobbering in my ear, mother fucker! What the hell is wrong with you?" he asked.

"Al, the players, the players," I said frantically. "I think they have some drug dealers with them. I think they're doing lines up there."

Al shook me off of his shoulder. "Are you for real?" he asked. "Get back to your line. You have a job here. What are you going to do if some rascals roll up? You're my front line. You watch the door." He pushed me back towards the door. I began to walk back to the door, shook up, nervous about the drugs and the obvious crime situation, when I glanced at the stage. A new dancer was up—tall and angular, soft, cocoa brown skin, with hair cut short and bleached blond. Another square, plain face. Disappointing. Obvious breast implants ballooned incredulously from a silvery-blue sequined top. The music started, and the dancer bent down and slid into a back-facing split. At that moment, the dancer's wardrobe experienced a major malfunction. Her thong popped all the way off, and her penis flopped out. Her penis.

A couple of the players let out loud roars. Chairs flew across the room as some of the guys jumped up and started to holler. Other guys looked visibly nervous, but said nothing as they slowly edged towards the door. Al sprang from table to table, trying to calm the patrons. I really couldn't believe it, but now it all made sense. My eyes ran over the dancers that had been on the players' laps, the dancers in the back row of the stage, the dancers waiting at the bar, the dancers back in the wings. They all had that tall, lanky, slightly muscled look. They all had narrow hips. They all had obvious breast implants. They all had hard, angular faces. They were all

guys. They were all guys. I was bouncing for a tranny strip

club.

A couple of the players were getting really mad. They

were pushing around the dancers and screaming at Al. The

bartender caught my eye, grabbed the phone, and ducked

under the bar. He was obviously calling the cops. I checked the

time on my cell phone. 44 minutes, 58 seconds until I could

count on police backup. Shit.

What was my job in this scenario? Think. What had Al

said? Hustle the dancers out, and call the cops. Let's see. The

bartender was already calling the cops. Cross that one off the

list. Hustle the dancers out. Hmm, front door or back door?

Which would the dancers prefer? An evil little voice in my

head whispered, *Oh Danny, you know thesth guysth love the

back door*. "Shut up!" I hissed to myself. "That's just a

stereotype!"

I grabbed two of the she-males and yanked them towards the back of the club, pushing them to the fire exit. I pushed my way back through the crowd, and grabbed a couple more that had been sitting with the players. One of the players was getting loud with the dancers, yelling and trying to grab his money back. The dancer bitch-slapped him across the face and jammed the roll of cash into his bra. The player pushed the dancer back a couple of feet and pulled a gun out of his baggy pants pocket. Time slowed down and the blood roared in my ears. I was way, way too close to the dancer. I was way too close to the gun. The football player was yelling something that I couldn't hear or comprehend. My attention was fixated on the gun and the certain death that it carried. If he swings just a few inches too far I'm dead, I thought. Dead. Dead. Dead.

The club door flew open and banged into the wall. The second scuffler was there in his Redskins jersey, brandishing an enormous firearm. I dropped to the floor, pissed myself, and began marine-crawling to the fire exit. "oh god oh god oh god" I chanted, "oh god oh god..."

"DROP YOUR WEAPONS," boomed a voice over a megaphone. "POLICE. DROP YOUR WEAPONS." I curled into a ball on the floor under a table. A dancer was curled up next to me, tears streaking his mascara down his cheek, snot leaking out of his nose. He sobbed a little and hiccupped. I pulled a travel-pack of Kleenex out of my jeans' pocket and handed it to him.

The player dropped the clip out of his gun, slowly laid the gun onto the table, and put his hands up. The second scuffler rushed up, knocked away the gun, flashed a badge hanging from a chain around his neck, and began to cuff him. "You dumb bitch," he said to me. "Letting in the dealers. I'll need to talk to you. You've got some explaining to do. Of course, like everyone else here, you DO have the right to stay silent, you drug-promoting tranny lover. And you DO have the right to an attorney, who will want to advise you not to drop the soap, unless you are a taker, not a giver. Do you have any questions?"

I did not. I got cuffed and questioned, just like everyone else. All of my cash got taken away and labeled as "EVIDENCE." Ha! Easy come, easy go. In the end, I wasn't arrested, but the club was shut down under suspicion of drug trafficking and male prostitution. So much for my big job. After a long night with the police, I finally got to go home.

I got home from that fiasco just as the sun was coming up. I was tired and needed to blow off some steam. I needed to relieve my stress and just relax. Given what I had just gone through, sexual release was the last avenue I wanted to take for stress relief. I didn't want to think about scantily-clad women again for the rest of my life—or at least for the next two days. What the hell, I figured. I'll go for a run.

I first became a runner in high school, and generally found it to be a great way to work up a sweat and think through my problems. When I run, I start with an empty mind, just chugging along. Part way through the run, I find my mind picks up a mantra and chants it to the cadence of my stride. It's usually pretty inspiring. I imagine myself as a great athlete, my feet thumping to the rhythm of "*climb* the *moun*·tain, *climb* the *moun*·tain" or "*not* too *far* now, *you* can *do* it. *Not* too *far* now, *you* can *do* it!"

Today I laced up my shoes and stretched on my front steps, leaning against the hand rail. It briefly creaked. Then, the rail suddenly snapped off in my hands, and I pitched over off the porch, headfirst into the azalea bushes.

"AAUGH!" I yelled. Shit! This house was just unbelievably awful. I crawled out of the bush, and shook my head. Cautiously, I stretched out on the sidewalk, and began a wobbly, slow pace down the block. I tried to let my mind empty out, but it was just stuffed full of the horrible events that I had lived in the last few days and weeks. Who knew that life could be so bad? I jogged around the corner and slightly down the hill. My life just sucked, and there were no two ways about it. As I jogged along, the neighborhood dads kissed their wives goodbye and drove off to their jobs. Neighborhood moms were driving their kids to school. Older neighbors were power-walking as couples. Everyone I saw had something to live for. I had nothing. My legs got warm. Birds chirped overhead. My mind began to empty out, my thoughts swam. I jogged. One two three four. One two three four. I slowly became aware of today's mantra, as I jogged along. "*One* two *three* four. *Eat* a *bu*llet. *One* two *three* four. *Eat* a *bu*llet. *One* two *three* four. *Eat* a *bu*llet."

Whoa. That's a place that I didn't want to go. I stopped abruptly and looked at the sky. A V-shaped formation of geese honked and flapped overhead. I've never been depressive in my life, or even very introspective. Hearing my brain subconsciously advocate suicide was new for me. I decided to forget about the run and just walk home. At least when I walk my mind doesn't randomly wander into scary places.

As I walked up the block, some of my older neighbors were clustered on the sidewalk opposite my house, pointing at the broken porch rail and speaking animatedly to each other. As I strolled up, they abruptly broke off from the conversation and scurried back into their houses. Gauzy curtains commenced twitching as I put my key into the front door.

When I walked through the door, my cell phone was ringing on the counter. Too sweaty to put it on my cheek—I punched up speaker phone. "Hey, Danny here," I said. God, I hoped it was a job interview, for a real job.

"Hey Sweetheart, it's Amaya calling," said a soft female voice. Amaya. Amaya. Oh no! my former coworker, rendered unemployed due to a mix of my incompetence, her willingness to help a stranger, and the inexplicable cloud of bad luck that hovered over me and any employment opportunity that passed my way.

"Oh, Amaya, how are you doing," I greeted her lamely. "How's it going with you? Did you find a new job?"

"Oh sure, sugar, I told you I was going to work in my cousin's 7-11. He put me to work right away, it's not too bad. How're you doing? You doing ok? Find a new job?"

"Um, sort of." I sighed. "I had a job but then there was a police raid, so it was another bust."

"Police raids are the worst, sweetie."

"Yeah," I sighed, "so..."

"Anything else going on? You sound bummed out. Come on," she cajoled, "let's hear it. You tell me yours, I'll tell you mine."

"My house is all screwed up!" I burst out. "My wiring needs to get fixed, I can't afford an electrician, all I have to eat is microwave burritos, but my microwave dies whenever they are half-cooked. My sink is broken, and I can't afford a plumber. I just broke my front porch, and now the world can see what a dump I live in."

"Not too bad," Amaya congratulated me. "That's the old saying, right? 'You don't own your house, your house owns you.' You know, you can come on down here to the 7-11 and use our microwave if that's all you have to eat. It's ok."

"I might have to take you up on that," I said. "That, or switch to Top Ramen. I'm not really a cook, you know."

"Sweetie, it's a skill. More you practice, the better you'll get. It'll get better. And if you come down here and use the microwave, I'll teach you some recipes. Don't worry."

"Amaya, did you have some news? Anything I can do for you?" I offered.

"Yes, I've talked to Judy a couple of times. The person who stole my receipts never looked up, so they never got her on the security camera. If you can possibly think of what she might look like, that might help. I won't get the job back, but I would feel better if the thief is caught. Otherwise, the store has also contacted the credit card companies, and the companies are supposed to be monitoring the cards. Judy gave me a little more information, between you and me, the cards include two Mastercards, last four digits 2777 and 6189, and a Visa ending 4244."

"Ok, hang on. Let me write that down." I looked around the kitchen and tried to find a piece of paper. Nothing. Pen? Nothing. I scrabbled through a couple of junky drawers, and found nothing. "Hang on Amaya." I could not believe it—not a thing to write with. When Lacey was still around, there was a pad of paper and a pen in every room, and an extra hanging on the fridge by a magnet. She was so anal about paper and pens. Where the hell had all my paper gone? Shit. I couldn't keep Amaya waiting. I grabbed a dirty fork out of the sink, and used it to gouge the information into our Tuscan-style, terra-cotta painted kitchen wall. M2777, M6189, V4244. Not that it told me anything. I stared at the ugliness of my wall, and then shook my head. What had we been thinking? Why had we chosen such an awful paint color? Forget the crummy job the developer had done, and the Chinese drywall reputation. I could never sell this house, because it was too fucking ugly for anyone to seriously consider buying. I don't know, maybe it had potential for a would-be slum lord.

"They said that if they can catch the person using the cards on the Internet they might be able to track down who it is based on where the ordered goods are shipped, if they are shipped to a live address. But, if you can think of anything that might help, there's a reward, from the store and from the credit card companies, and it totals to $25,000 between the two for information that will lead to an arrest."

"Wow, that's a lot of money!" I exclaimed. "I wish I could help. I'll think a little on it, and see if I can remember anything. Thanks, Amaya."

"No problem, sugar. You take care now. And don't forget to come on down here with your burritos. Bye now." The phone went silent. I stared at it, then stared at the numbers on my wall again. M2777, M6189, V4244. I wondered why Amaya had bothered to ask what the numbers were. Oh well. I was still sweaty and gross from my night of getting pinned down and cuffed on the floor of the strip club, and from my abortive run. I stripped off my clothes and threw them into the washing machine, and started a load. Then, I headed upstairs naked, and got into the shower. It was nice for the first minute, until the water started squirting and spraying randomly everywhere. The shower head started making a repetitive clunking noise. I looked up in disbelief—the nozzle was jerking up and down by half-inches in concert with a clunking sound in the pipes. Getting out, I wrapped a towel around myself and stared at the broken sink—same clunking sound. I followed the noise down to the laundry room in the basement. The washing machine was set on "warm"—and appeared to be unable to dispense hot and cold simultaneously. The water was abruptly dispensing hot, then cold, then hot, then cold—and every pipe in the house was shaking accordingly. Fury built up in me. I bellowed in rage and punched the wall. FUCK! A big gaping hole was now in the wall, and my hand killed. It was scraped and started to swell. I flipped the washing machine cycle to "cold", went back upstairs, and got back into my shower. I scrubbed off, shaved, and stood under the water until it turned cold. I turned it off, toweled off, and collapsed into bed. *Day is done*, I thought. *Day is done.* I went to sleep.

CHAPTER SEVEN

I spent the weekend trying to think whether I could remember anything from the night I was fired from Blow-Mart, but I really came up with a blank. I did take Amaya up on the offer of the microwave, and spent a fair amount of time hanging around the 7-11 that weekend. As a result, when Monday morning rolled around, I smelled a little like bean burritos, but otherwise was in good shape to roll back into DOES in search of another job.

My career counselor at DOES, Pam, wasn't thrilled to see me, and it wasn't just my smell that she objected to. She especially wasn't thrilled to learn that I had made two job contacts last week and still remained unemployed. "Okay," she said, "we can authorize direct deposit of your unemployment benefits into your account. But I do have another opportunity for you, with a local small business owner. This one will count as your first job contact for the week. I thought it would be good for you, given your skillset. Let me know if it works out."

I looked on the reference card and sighed. Uncle Jimmy's Pizzeria.

Uncle Jimmy's is a local pizza shop, with a flagship location in Northeast DC, that has mysteriously garnered enough success to open up a couple more locations around the beltway. Uncle Jimmy's proudly undersells all competitors. I don't know what full-price is on a pie from Uncle Jimmy's, but every special on his TV commercials sells for $5.99, including toppings. I'm not sure how he does it, unless the cheese is made from re-purposed industrial waste and his pepperoni from sliced-up dog shit. That wouldn't surprise me, given how the pizzas taste. Uncle Jimmy also guarantees that their pizzas are delivered within 30 minutes or the order is free.

"How does this make good use of my skillset?" I asked Pam. "Do they need a business manager? Can I run some spreadsheets for them to analyze potential expansion into new markets? Do they need help writing a business plan to get a loan?"

"Danny, this job would use your driving skills more than anything," Pam said. "You have a clean driving record and your own car, and both are required to fill this particular position."

"You mean it's for pizza delivery?" I couldn't believe it. "What does it pay? Minimum wage?"

"Give it a try," she encouraged me. "It's evening hours, so it leaves your days free to look for a more suitable position. You also make tips, and that can add up. I know a lot of people who keep driving pizza delivery even after they get a day job, just so they can keep the extra money. You know, for holiday gifts and vacations and such."

Hmmm, tips. Tips didn't sound so bad. I guess that I could live with tips.

"Ok, I'll apply," I said. "In the meantime, my cash is pretty tight. You said that my unemployment is getting direct-deposited?"

"That's right, the money should be in your account tomorrow," Pam said. "I'll call these guys and let them know to expect you tonight."

"Hey, thanks Pam. I'll head out there. You take care," I said, and rolled out of DOES.

Tomorrow couldn't come soon enough. I was out of money and out of food. If I got the pizza job and got lucky, someone would do a prank pizza order and I could get a free dinner off of it. Otherwise, I might be hungry until my unemployment check got deposited. Hmm. Maybe I should make my own luck, I thought, and use my cell phone to call in a phony order myself. I idly wondered whether Uncle Jimmy's had caller ID.

I drove out to the location listed on the reference card. The restaurant was Uncle Jimmy's newest location, out in Tyson's Corner, Virginia. This location was a tiny, glass-enclosed store-front in a new strip mall. Customers could walk in and order or pick up a phoned-in order from a chest-high counter. No seating was available. A blond, frizzy-haired teenaged girl was behind the counter. She smiled, and a mouthful of metal jangled out at me.

"Uncle Jimmy's loves to bring your piece of pizza," she chirped out at me. "Can I take your order?" Her face looked like a pizza. Fascinating. The manager, Abdul, came up from the manager's office and waved her off, clearly expecting me. Abdul was wearing a shocking yellow and blue uniform top, emblazoned on the left pocket with Uncle Jimmy's smiling-faced logo.

"Hi Danny, glad to meet you. I'm really glad DOES was able to send us someone so quickly—we have a new investor coming to visit the franchise tonight, and it was going to look pretty bad if we were backed up on deliveries. You're hired. We'll do the paperwork at the end of your shift. Look, let's just go over the basics? We do deliveries and take-out only, no eat-in. Wash your hands whenever you come in to the restaurant, here at the sink. Take orders here at the counter if you are on register, or here for the phone. Punch the order into the register, and it pops up on the monitor back in the kitchen for the cook to prepare. You need to wear your uniform top and sun visor whenever you are here or out delivering."

"But I'm going to be delivering at night," I observed. "Sun visor?"

"Look, I know, but it's part of the uniform. If people don't see it through the peephole, they might not open the door. It's important to get the customers to open the door as soon as possible, because if the pizza isn't in their hands within 30 minutes of placing the order, the pizza is free."

"Thirty minutes, got it. How do we make sure that happens?"

"We have a strict policy on our delivery areas. We've taken traffic patterns, time of day, and so on into account to determine what our delivery zone is. If the caller doesn't live in our zone, we let them know that we can't take their order. You'll need to get to know the delivery zone, though, because some of the neighborhoods are tricky."

"Oh, that's no problem," I bragged. "I have Nav in my car. I'll just punch in the addresses."

"Hey, that's great. So, you go to the kitchen, pick up the delivery slip, check that you have everything on it—pizza? Salad? Drinks? Don't forget anything, it's all subject to that 30 minute rule."

"Check the slip. Got it," I parroted.

"Great. Look, let's go over the rules of pizza delivery. First, always knock sharply on the door three times. When the customer opens the door, you have to announce the slogan. 'Uncle Jimmy's loves to bring your piece of pizza!' Then present the slip, confirm the items to be delivered, and the total. TAKE THE MONEY FIRST, then hand over the food. If you give the food over first, they might slam the door and lock it, and then you are screwed. You have to pay the bill when you get back, and if they stiff you, the cost of the pizza comes out of your pocket."

"Holy shit," I said. "What if I get stiffed all night? I could end up negative!"

"That's why you always take the money first. If they don't pay, you can just bring the pizza back here and we can write it off. You know, throw it into the freezer--we give the undelivered pizzas to the homeless shelter. But if you come back with no pizza, some one has to pay. Look, we have to make it that way, that way we know drivers can't just call in phony orders to get free pizza for their friends."

Damn. Clearly there was no way that I was going to get a free pizza out of this job. Not unless I moved into the homeless shelter. "Alright, well, sounds like that covers the basics. Am I ready to start delivering?"

"Not quite. I haven't given you the Golden Rule yet."

"I thought that was the rule about getting the money first."

"That's a good rule of thumb, but not the Golden Rule. The Golden Rule is, never go into the house." I gave him a quizzical look.

"Why would I go into the house?"

"Who the hell knows? But drivers sometimes do, and I'm telling you, it never works out. There is no faster way to get accused of theft or malfeasance than to go inside the customer's house. No matter what happens, just stay on the front porch."

"Ok, got it," I said. "Where do I pick up the pizzas?"

Abdul took me back into the kitchen, where he introduced me to the cook and showed me where the pre-packaged salads and refrigerated drinks were kept. He also showed me where the order slips were, and the hot and cold insulated bags for delivering the food. "Everything good, Danny? Any questions?"

"Yeah, how much do I make?"

"You make $8.25 an hour, plus if you write down your mileage we reimburse you on your gas. Oh, and if you make any tips, you can keep those, but don't forget to keep track of them so you can put them on your tax return. The IRS has a real stick up its ass about underreported tips."

Good to know. Wow, do I ever hate the IRS. If there's any government agency I hate and fear more than the SEC, it's the IRS. Let me tell you about the fucking IRS... well, maybe that's a story for another time. Back at Uncle Jimmy's, Abdul went back into the manager's office, and I was left in the kitchen with the cook. I wondered what had happened to the last driver. What the hell? Why not ask the cook. Break the ice with my new coworker. I looked at him dubiously. He had earbuds stuffed in his ears and the volume turned way up. I tried to catch his attention by saying "hi," and then by waving my hands, but he didn't see or hear me. I finally had to resort to tapping his shoulder.

"Yeah man?"

"Hi. Um. Hi." I was drawing a blank. I guess I wasn't sure how to start talking to a guy whose pants were bagging down and belted in just above his knees, and who was wearing a backwards, upside down pizza visor.

"Are you asking me a for a date?"

Oh shit. "NO! no. I'm just..." A total fucktard. I'm an idiot. I couldn't spit out a sentence. Agony... he was staring at me and I was turning purple. "I'm..." I cleared my throat. "I'm wondering why the last driver quit."

"Oh, he didn't quit. He was put in jail."

"Jail?" I choked out. Flashbacks from Beauties raced through my mind. "Was it job related?"

"Jail. No, it was personal, but it meant he didn't make it to work. Kind of beyond his control, but still a terminating event. He called up one night and told Abdul that he was going to be late. Then he called a little later and said he was in jail. Then, he called a little after that and asked if we would bail him out, because his mom wouldn't do it and neither would his girlfriend. We didn't bail him out, so he wasn't able to drive that shift. I don't think that counts as quitting."

"Oh." I commented lamely. Not a lot to say about that. It seemed like a natural place to euthanize what was left of the conversation. The good news was, a pizza order came in and I got to stop trying to talk.

My first couple of orders went fine. I silently congratulated myself for having a navigation system in my car. How the hell could anyone deliver pizzas without Nav? I zipped around, delivering pies in record time. My first house, I got tipped a buck fifty. The second house, three dollars! I had only been working for an hour and an half, and I already had almost five dollars cash. I wouldn't have to phone in a phony pizza order, after all—not that it would do me any good, anyway. I could afford some Taco Bell.

I drove back to the restaurant, and a third order was waiting. "Hey Danny," snickered the cook, "have fun with this one. We have a famous customer." I looked at the address and the time of the order, and panicked internally. The house was pretty far away, and I only had 10 minutes to get there. I hustled out to the car, punched the address into my Nav, and started to drive.

Shit! Shit. This house was too far away. Why would they accept an order from such a distant house? There was no way it would be possible to get a cooked pizza to this house in under thirty minutes. I raged at a red light, pounded the horn and flashed headlights when the driver ahead didn't move quick enough, cut off some other drivers, and generally congratulated myself on not getting pulled over or arrested.

The address required a fairly early turn off of the main road, followed by what seemed like miles of wandering through the giant subdivision from hell. "Forest Knolls" the sign read. No forest nor knolls were in sight anywhere. Instead, I wound through recently platted new construction, huge houses on miniscule lots spaced just feet apart. Left, left, around a curve, right, left... I wound the car further and further into hell, anxiety creasing my forehead. My neck and shoulders tightened up as I hunched over the wheel, following the calm, vapid directions of the navigational computer's electronic voice. The time ticked down as I drew closer and closer. God, I could see the pinpoint of my destination on the Nav screen. The route map indicated a neat spiral into the address. Almost there... almost there... There! I screeched up to the house, ran full out up the walk, and pounded on the door.

"Uncle Jimmy's loves to bring your piece of pizza!" I screamed, sweat trickling down the side of my face. The door swung open, and my jaw dropped.

Standing before me was a vision of brunette beauty, tucked into skinny jeans and a crop-top bustier. "Wow," she sighed through glossy lips, "my pizza." I stared into her cleavage and garbled out a strangled reply. "Thanks," she murmured, taking it from me. "Want to come in for your tip?"

Hello, Penthouse forum. I could not believe it. This was the stuff of legends. Who ever thought that a pizza delivery guy could actually get taken inside and tipped by hotness? No wonder Uncle Jimmy's took orders from this house. Who could turn her down? Who gave a shit about a free pizza when the price was five minutes with this lady?

"So," she said, peaking inside the box. "Where's the coke?"

"Oh, I'm sorry," I said. "Oh, Jeez, I'm so sorry. It's my first night. I didn't see that there was a soft drink for the order. I'll go back and get it. You don't have to tip me…"

I trailed of as she giggled. "You aren't the usual guy," she said. "He always brings my coke. And I'm always so very, very grateful…" she swayed up to me. Oh, God. She smelled so good. Her skin smelled like perfume, and lotion. She DEFINITELY looked like a woman. No she-male here. I touched her arm. She smiled at me. Her eyes crinkled, and she popped open the button on my jeans. The zipper dragged down, and she sank to her knees. Oh. My. God.

My eyes closed, and I prepared to enter heaven. "You don't have to tip me," I mumbled again. She snickered.

"Oh, but I LOVE giving tips," she said.

I was going to love this job. She started to tug my boxers down, when suddenly, the front door banged open.

"What the hell is going on here!" hollered an older guy. "What are you doing to my daughter!?"

Daughter? That was it. No words, time to go. "You bastard!" he raged, leaping after me. "She's only seventeen! You're a monster! I'll see you in court!" I ran out of the house as fast as I had run up to it, and squealed out of the driveway as fast as I could, hoping beyond hope that the guy hadn't notice what kind of car I was driving or the plate.

Damn it. Damn. Damn. Damn. This is the worst situation any guy could find himself in. She looked like a grownup! She looked eighteen. She looked twenty three! She didn't look seventeen. I didn't come on to her! I didn't do anything! I was a victim here. Oh, man, what was I going to do? Just because some coked-up little princess got friendly with the pizza delivery guy, I might have to go to jail. I didn't even get lucky. Instead, I got stiffed on the pizza, and stiffed on the tip.

After I made my way out of the subdivision, I slowed down a little. No need to drive wildly or otherwise call legal attention to myself. The drive back to Uncle Jimmy's was a time for sober reflection. Where had I gone wrong? Clearly, the cook had some inside knowledge. He had laughed and made a comment, and I had made no attempt to share in his institutional knowledge. Instead, I had just bolted ahead with the project, and the result was a negative outcome. I hadn't carefully checked the delivery slip. That meant that I was uncertain of what items were included in the scope of delivery. Finally, I had broken that most important rule, I had entered her home, and thus made myself vulnerable to her advances, and thus vulnerable to the collateral damage—getting caught when her dad walked in.

I slunk back in to Uncle Jimmy's. Not unexpectedly, the manager Abdul was waiting for me. "Danny," he said. "Danny. The guy at your last delivery called. He was very upset."

"I know," I said. "Look, I can explain. I'm really sorry, but it's all her fault."

"Her fault?" he asked. "How is it her fault? The customer is always right."

My chest grew tight. I wasn't sure where he was going with this, but there was no question that it wouldn't work out well for me. "I... because she said..."

"Look, the guy called up and made it very clear that they weren't paying for the pizza because the pie got there in 37 minutes. That's seven minutes late. Look, I know that house is on the border of undeliverable, but the last driver was always able to make it there in time, and they order pizza almost every night. We can't afford to give away free pies every night. I'm really sorry, but we can't keep you on if you can't timely deliver to our regular customers. I'm going to have to let you go. I really hate to do this, especially with the new investor here."

I caught sight of someone in the manager's office. I cringed as he turned and caught sight of me as well, in my Uncle Jimmy's visor and garish uniform shirt. "Danny? What the hell are you doing?" he asked. Oh God.

"Hi Jason," I sighed. There were no words.

"Hey, Abdul, can I have a moment with Danny in the office?"

"Oh yes, sir," Abdul toadied up to my brother. "Of course, it's your office, you are the investor here, sir." He cast a dark look on me, as though to warn me from doing anything to taint the investor, the office, or the company in general. Jason pulled me into the office and slammed the door closed behind us.

"Danny, what the hell is going on here? Why are you driving pizza delivery for my restaurant? What the fuck? Look, let me give you a little money, ok? This isn't right. I can help you by until you get back on your feet, you don't need to do this shit."

Something welled up inside of me—anger, and maybe some pride. Ok, a lot of pride. I had wanted to ask Jason for money a few weeks ago. I had even gone over to his house intending to do so. God knows he has plenty of it, and could give me all I needed and more without feeling the pinch. But I didn't want to take from him, even before I started working with DOES, and now that I was three failed jobs into the job hunt, I'd be damned if I'd take his money. I knew he would try to insist, though. Crap, how could I *avoid* taking his money?

"Oh, this?" I gestured lamely at the ugly uniform. "This is just a cover. You know, for my real job."

"Your real job? What's that? Does it involve letters to Penthouse?" he asked eagerly. Wow, sometimes I wonder if Jason is really my brother, but I'm ashamed to say that comments like that reaffirm that we truly share DNA. "Will you be going to a special awards ceremony in Las Vegas for this work?" That's my brother. Class all the way.

"No, I'm, um, undercover."

"You're a COP? Does Dad know? Wait, you're in deep cover, and you're going to pull a sting operation on Dad, right?"

"No, I'm still in my old industry. I, that is…"

Jason gave me a puzzled look. "Insurance? Undercover insurance?"

"That's right. I'm, um, investigating insurance fraud." Ugh, lamest line ever. "You know, sometimes people will get into wrecks on purpose, for insurance fraud, so I'm working in a … driving-intensive scenario for information gathering purposes."

"Oh!" Jason smiled. "Clever! Very nice! Hope it segues back into office work, but glad that you've got a gig going. Does, um, Abdul know? Should I lean on him to get you back on the job?"

"Oh, no, no…" I demurred. "No, that would flag me. No, um, for verisimilitude I should get 'fired' in this circumstance." I dropped quotes around the word "fired" with my fingers. "The insurance company will place me in a different scenario. That way, I maximize my information gathering. The variety gives me an opportunity to validate the model by sampling an adequate volume of data." Blah blah blah. But Jason was nodding and smiling, so my bullshit was working.

"I get it, I get it. Very elaborate! Good job, brother. Alright, 'YOU'RE FIRED!'" He yelled, then giggled. "Get the hell out of here. Grab a pizza on your way. Whatever you want, on the house." He grabbed me into a bear hug, then ushered me out of the office.

CHAPTER EIGHT

I was driving home from the pizza delivery fiasco, free shitty pizza on the front seat next to me. Clearly, pizza delivery was not going to be the optimal way to exploit my only real asset (my car) for income. While idling at a light, I glanced at the car next to me. "BE LIKE ME!" was printed across the side. "MAKE MONEY IN YOUR COMMUTE!" It listed a website underneath.

I had heard about companies like this, on the news one night. Companies looking for advertising exposure will pay to have their information spray-painted onto commuter's cars. The thought is, that while office-goers are creeping in to work in the city in heavy traffic at 2 miles per hour, like cancerous pilgrims crawling towards Mecca, they could stare at Mega-maid, dog walker, and plumber advertisements for hours on end. Theoretically this approach might result in an increase in people wanting services from said providers. I don't know why the advertisers think that people are receptive to advertising at those moments. I know that when I'm stuck in morning traffic, my mind tends to think about Michael Douglas in "Falling Down", just getting out of his car and going on a violent, armed rampage. Maybe that's just me, feeling my blood pressure rise and hating every car around me. Maybe other commuters are calmer. Personally, those are also the moments when I fantasize and wish that my car come equipped with a one-use only roof rocket.

A roof-rocket, in my fantasy, is a special feature installed on the roof of my car. I could use it once, and only once, to annihilate any single car in traffic. The roof rocket isn't like an airbag. It can't be deployed and reloaded. Therefore, if I had one, I would have to use great discretion in determining which asshole driver was deserving of my wrath.

Sometimes I think that perhaps the roof rocket should be carefully controlled, with a dual key authentication (like the president needs if he wants to nuke some awful country). On the other hand, nobody ever rides in my car except me, and it's impossible for me to drive at the same time I'm turning both ignition switches to deploy the roof rocket. Maybe I should start picking people up from the car pool line, to give me a second set of hands in those crucial moments for initiating and deploying the roof rocket. But then, what if they disagreed with my arms policy and opposed the use of force on my fellow drivers? No, it had better be just one big red button—but not installed on my steering wheel. Too accessible, and too tempting. Maybe inside the glove compartment. If I had one, I like to think I would save my roof rocket for the day when some asshole is booming his bass into my hangover. KA-BOOM! Roof rocket successfully deployed. It would make my headache worse, but guaranteed the roof rocket would provide a deterrent to would-be noise polluters. Let's get real, though. If I had a roof rocket, it would be used against whatever creep cut me off in traffic, ten minutes after it was installed on my car.

Oh well, back to making money by driving. Figuring it was worth a try, I noted the website and logged on when I got home. I chowed down my shitty pizza, brushed my teeth, and dropped into bed.

I woke up Tuesday morning, feeling inexplicably happy. I rolled over onto my side and felt around. Nope, no lady in bed with me. Hmmm. I shuffled out of bed and downstairs to the kitchen. My refrigerator held half a bar of butter, two lonely eggs, and the remnants of my Uncle Jimmy's pizza. I shuddered at the thought of cold Uncle Jimmy's for breakfast, glanced at the microwave, and wondered whether it would hold up to reheating pizza. Not likely. I scrambled up the eggs and wolfed them down. Not too bad—only a few little broken shells crunched in my teeth.

I still couldn't think what was making me feel so cheerful. I had no job, and had only made one job contact this week, so a trip back down the Orange line was inevitable. I had no money. I had... MONEY!

Pam had promised that my unemployment benefits would be direct deposited today. I did some quick math. After I paid my power bill, phone bill, and gassed up the car, I might have fifty bucks left to spend on food. Mmmm... my eyes glazed over and I drooled a little at the thought of eating something other than takeout pizza and burritos.

I grabbed a quick shower, dressed in Levi's and a T-shirt, then popped onto my laptop to check my online banking. There it was! There it was! I did a little dance. I had money.

First things first. I shuffled through my bills. Mortgage—trash. Electric—keep. Gas—keep. Phones—cell and home. Which to pay? *Home phone means internet*, I told myself. *Do you want to surf the net at the library?* I shuddered again, and promised myself I'd pay the cell phone next go around. I raced through online bill pay, then grabbed my keys and headed out.

I drove out to the Exxon. $4.24 a gallon for gas! My eyes strayed a little down the street to the Liberty gas station··

$3.97 a gallon. "Sorry baby," I whispered to my Beemer, "but someday Daddy will make it all better." I drove a half-block further to gas up at Liberty, and hit my next dilemma. $3.97 for octane 93 super primo gasoline... or $3.77 for the 87 octane rating. My eyes misted over, and I half-covered the sob choking out as I punched the 87 button. "I wish I didn't have to do this to you," I sobbed softly, "I promise I'll by you the good stuff next time!" The woman at the next pump gave me a funny look, and I saw her fumble with her keys to prime her pepper spray. I ducked into my car and closed the door, staring at the steering column until the tank was full.

Off next to the 'Teet. Gotta love Harris Teeter, but I don't always love the prices. It's big, clean, and beautiful, with lots of selection and great items, but you pay. You pay. On the way to the 'Teet, I passed a smaller grocery store that I had never shopped in—Grand Mart. I wondered what their prices were like. I pulled into the lot, walked in, and blinked. It was a journey into the Third World. The grocery carts were banged up. There was no coffee bar or hot foods market. No floral section. Yep, it was for certain, poor people shop here.

Grand Mart had tons of produce. I wasn't sure what to do with most of the vegetables, but apples were seventy cents a pound, so I filled a produce bag with apples. Canteloupe, a dollar fifty each. Sure. Eggs were ninety-seven cents a carton. These prices were certainly better than Harris Teeter, but the ambience was crap.

I made my way through the store, throwing pasta, tuna, mayonnaise, OJ, and toilet paper into my cart. I wasn't sure what to think of the exotic Asian, Middle Eastern, and Hispanic spices, so I passed them by. The meat section was full of fascinating cuts of pork and beef, various animal innards that I'd never heard of or considered eating before. I still wouldn't consider eating most of it. Pass. I grabbed some ground beef, held my nose as I passed the odorous sea food display, and turned back into the aisles.

Small tub of coffee, laundry soap—Tide or Purex? I'd never heard of Purex before, but it was five dollars cheaper than Tide. I guiltily looked at the other cleaning products. The housekeepers had been let go when I lost my job, and I hadn't done much with the housekeeping since. I didn't even know what cleaning products I already had. I promised to myself that I'd take inventory and get cleaning, then walked on. Cold case—I had just over fifty bucks to spend. I mentally tallied what I had in the basket and winced—it was going to be an alcohol-free week.

I checked out and rolled out the door, then realized that was the end of the line. It must have been an anti-theft policy, but the grocery carts were blocked from leaving the vicinity of the store by a huge metal rail all along the front sidewalk. I saw other shoppers standing guard over their grocery carts while family members brought around the cars to load in front of the metal rail. Well, how was I supposed to get my bags to the car? If I left the cart to get my car, what if someone stole my groceries? The store was clearly patronized by poor losers whose desperation knew no bounds.

I looped all of my plastic grocery bags over my fingers, lifted them up, and prayed that my eggs wouldn't break. Halfway to my car, I realized that the tight plastic loops were cutting off blood to my fingers. I hurried, half-stumbling to my car, but then couldn't get my keys out of my pocket. I tried to unloop the bags from my fingers, the tips swelling and turning purple like grapes. Finally, I got the bags off and the keys out. I loaded up the trunk and got behind the wheel.

As I turned on the car, my Bluetooth chirped an incoming call. I punched the hands-free button on my steering column, and the call came in over my car stereo speakers.

"Hello?"

"Hi!" bubbled out a very happy female voice. "This is Sandy calling. May I speak to Danny?"

"You've got him," I said. "How may I help you?"

"Well, Danny, do you need a little extra money?"

"Ye·es," I said cautiously. She was a little too happy.

"Well, do you drive your car during rush hour on a major freeway every day?"

I used to. I guess I could pick up carpoolers and run up and down the freeway twice a day, if it would make me some money. "Yes, I drive up the 395 every morning and evening."

"Wow, Danny. That's great. Did you know that you could make tons of money, doing nothing different whatsoever, just by driving your car to and from work every day, just like usual?"

There was no use in telling this woman that I'd been canned. She was kind of creepy and pushy, like a timeshare salesperson. I knew there had to be a catch, but I was desperate to know just how much money I could make (not likely much) and how awful the catch would be.

"Well, Sandy, that's what the car ad said, and that's why I called, but I'm not sure how this all works."

Well, she boiled it right down for me. I would have to hand my car over for a little less than a day. Her company would paint some other company's logo onto my car, and I would get paid for the promise of driving my car around in heavy traffic on a regular basis. The amount of compensation would be based on the size of the advertisement and the level of difficulty the advertising company had in getting some driver to accept their advertisements.

I assured Sandy that I would be down to have my car painted right away, and that I was interested in the maximum amount of remuneration possible. She took down some specifics—my name, address, make and model on the car, and so on, and gave me some directions on how to get to the shop. As I punched the steering column button to end the call, I could hear her gurgling her delight, over her assurances that I would not be sorry and that it was a great opportunity.

I swung by my house, unloaded all of the groceries, and got right back into my car. I couldn't believe that I was about to whore out my ride. It had been so good to me! So many fine ladies had turned in traffic to express that silent admiration. So many lipglossed lips had noiselessly cooed out through their window and mine, "I love your CAR..." And here I went, getting ready to debase it, just to get a little money. What the hell, a man's gotta eat.

The car shop was in Oxon Hill, Maryland. It's not too often that I cross over the Woodrow Wilson Bridge into Prince George's County. Most of my Maryland time is spent driving around Rockville and Potomac, visiting my family in very white, very Jewish neighborhoods. PG County isn't necessarily more ethnically diverse than Montgomery County—it's just a different ethnicity altogether. I get a little uncomfortable coming in on the south side of the beltway. There's a lot of crime in PG county, and I kind of feel like a target—pasty skinny white guy, driving a nice car. Again, my inner racist sprung out, and I had to speak to that nasty demon. *Don't fear,* I thought. *These are your brothers, not some others.* I drove fast, sweating a little that I might get lost. I found the paint shop, and pulled my car up into a service bay as the outdoor attendant, an older black man in a jumpsuit, waived me in. I walked down a hallway and into the lobby.

The whole building smelled oily and painty. A few plastic chairs were sitting around the waiting room, scuffed and peeling. The drywall had been painted off-white a long time ago, and it was randomly marked and dented. The floor was grungy linoleum tile. The restroom was just as dirty as the rest of the waiting area. I could tell, because the door had been ripped off the hinges at some point and just leaned against the wall next to the door frame.

"Danny?" Called out a bubbly female voice. In bounced Sandy, a short black lady with round perky breasts, an impossibly tiny waist, and a sproingy round butt, just as bubbly as her voice. She had braided hair, lots of eye makeup on, and dark red glossy lips. "Hiya! I'm so glad you came by. We have a great company for you, a really cute advertisement, and your car is going to look really great. Do you want to go over your paperwork?"

"Nah, that's ok, where do I sign?" I asked.

"No problem! That's here, and here" she pointed, "initial here, here, and here, and sign one more time here."

I signed and signed until she was done pointing. "How long is this going to take?" I asked. "Is there anything to do around here?"

"Well, I think we have a full-body ad for your car, and that could take quite a while." She said. "This isn't the greatest neighborhood for you to stroll around in, but you can take a seat here and wait for someone to come get you, or just wait for your car."

I waited. After a while, I dozed. It had been a long night, and I was really beat. My mind drifted, and I snoozed, dreaming weird dreams, of cars, and flying dollar bills, cars with giant thongs snapping off, a robot pizza trying to eat me, and roof rockets deploying. I woke a while later and shook off the dreams, then smirked to myself. This was so easy. The cash I would get would surely pay my cell phone and get me better gas for the car, maybe even some beer. It and unemployment would tide me over until I could get my resume out there and get a real job. I couldn't believe everyone wasn't doing this. It was so easy. Who cares if a mega-maid vacuum got painted onto my car door? I wouldn't have to see it. It wouldn't change my driving experience. It was free money. I had to hand it to myself; I was really starting to figure the world out. If I don't care what other people think, I could just walk away with the cash. Everyone else was just an idiot, asleep at the wheel, and passing on the cash. How much cash? I was sure it had to be as much as two or three hundred.

"Hey, Sandy?"

No answer. "Sandy?"

"Yes!" she came bubbling down the hallway. "Sorry, I was talking to the guys about your car. How can I help you, hon?"

"I was just wondering how much you were going to pay me for my car ad."

"Oh, that was in the paper work you signed. You still didn't look at that? You naughty boy. We're paying you $975 a month, just to drive around in your car!"

"Wait a minute," I said to Sandy. "$975 a month? I could buy another car for that. What am I doing in the car, muling drugs from Richmond up to Maryland?"

"Oh, NO!" she gasped, mascaraed eyes jumping open wide. She looked shocked. "Oh, gosh no! You said that you were willing to take the most money possible! We just have one particular client that is both interested in a full-body ad and that has been a little tough to place."

Why tough? I wondered. "What do you mean, tough? What's wrong with the company?"

"Well, it's a homeopathic company," she replied. "You know, some people don't think that homeopathic treatments are really medical care."

"That's because they're not," I said.

"Well, this company has all herbal treatments that they've been using to help people for over a hundred years. They think that with a little more exposure, they could really sell a lot of product. That's where you come in. Since you said that you were flexible to make the most money possible, I thought that this could be a great opportunity for you."

Sigh. Homeopathic treatments. That sounded like the dumb crap my ex-wife was into. Back when we were married, she was always bugging me to go with her to a couples yoga retreat, or to get his-and-her hot stone massages with herbal body wraps. She made me drink blended organic broccoli for breakfast once. It almost felt like a spiritual extension of Lacey, reaching across the miles to continue ruining my life post-divorce. But I needed the money, and there was no getting around that.

"Ok, I guess. When do I get to see my car?"

"Well, they've just finished it up, why don't you go take a peek?"

I walked back and down the hallway, and into the garage. There was my ride, but it was... pale green. Mostly pale green, with what looked like loopy ribbons or something in pale purple and pink. *I guess that's ribbons to tie up the herbs*, I mused to myself, and read the logo that was scripted on in more loopy, light blue letters. "Aunt... Judy's..." it was hard to read, it was so girly and curly. "All... Natural... Enemas... and ... Herbal... Suppositories... WHAAAAAAT!"

My eyes raced back up and frantically scanned the car again. Oh my God, no! What I thought were loopy ribbons were long, curled tubes ending in what was unmistakably an enema bag! UGH!

"Stop!" I screamed. "Stop! What are you doing to my car! I can't drive around in an enema car!"

"Look, you signed the consent, you have to drive the car now," said Sandy. Her voice was no longer bubbly or friendly. It had taken on a hard, businesslike edge. "You have contractually agreed to drive this car for a minimum of 90 days, in exchange for $975 per month. You have verified to us, subject to random audit, that you will drive 8 miles each way on the Virginia I-395 during peak rush hour at least 4 weekdays per week during that time period."

"I won't do it! I won't!" my voice shrieked. I sounded panicked and womanly. "I'll spray paint over it. I don't have to live like this!"

"You are of course free to do what you like with your own property," Sandy said. "But if you review the terms of your contract, you'll note that if you breach your contract by defacing the advertisement or failing to drive as agreed, you will have to reimburse our company for the cost of the custom paint job. In your case, that would amount to $4700."

I gasped. My chest tightened and it felt like all the air had left me. My eyes lost focus for a few moments. A few seconds later, I shook my head and realized that I was just screwed. There is no such thing as easy money. I had somehow duped myself into believing that everyone else was just a dummy, passing up free money, and that I was smarter than everyone else. Well, it just wasn't true. I wasn't smarter than anyone else, and the proof of that was the enema car that I would have to drive for the next 3 months.

Sandy assured me that they would direct deposit the first installment in the morning. I slunk out to my car and drove home in the twilight to cook myself dinner, and grab an early bedtime. Sleep eluded me again, and once again it was a late night watching re-runs on cable.

I woke up Wednesday morning, $975 richer but in a funk nonetheless. I had ruined my car, I still needed to head to DOES to get another job contact for the week, and my house was a filthy mess.

I hoped for a repeat scrambled egg breakfast, but had no clean pans. I popped two slices of bread into the toaster, poured juice and started coffee. A funny electric smell drifted into my nostrils. I turned back around to see sparks shooting out of the wall socket where the toaster was plugged in, and two flames shooting out of the bread slots. DAMMIT! I grabbed a mitt, yanked the whole toaster hard enough to pop the cord out of the wall, and dumped it into the sink.

So. Breakfast was two new slices of bread, eaten fresh. Yummy. Coffee and juice washed it down. I idly wondered if it was possible to keep eating for the rest of my life without ever cooking again.

I kept my promise to myself, and after breakfast began a search of the house for cleaning products. I finally located a stash of SoftScrub, Windex, Pledge, Formula 409, and other, less obvious cleaning products (vinegar?) in a cupboard in the laundry room. Moving them around to get a full inventory, I heard a strange clinking towards the back of the cupboard. I moved several more spray bottles out of the way, and stared dumb-founded at a small cache of bourbon and single malt that used to sit on my liquor cabinet. What the FUCK! My housekeepers had been stealing my liquor!

While rage and fury frothed through my brain, my inner voice reminded me that I had four bottles of quality hooch, when previously I had none. Best not to look that proverbial gift horse in the mouth. I took a quick slug of the bourbon, started a load of laundry, then carted the cleaning supplies up to the kitchen. I commenced scrubbing the house from top to bottom, getting into the groove, all Zen'd out scrubbing the toilet.

> Grimy ring around
> Brown stains the toilet bowl, ugh
> Scrubbing does no good.

The phone rang. I kept scrubbing and scrubbing, until I felt equilibrium. I headed into the kitchen to make lunch, and noticed the voicemail light blinking on my phone.

I listened to my voicemail, hoping it would be a recruiter, excited to see me for a real job opportunity. Instead, it was my mother, offering to host me for lunch and a guilt-trip. Sigh. I really needed a free lunch, but was it worth the guilt-trip? Not to mention having to take my shitty-looking car out of the garage during daylight hours.

"DANNY!" squealed my mother, forty-two minutes later. I was enveloped in a squishy, perfumed hug, my face pressed into her teased, hair-sprayed Heeb-hair. Mom has a head-full of kinky curls, kept dark by religious applications of Lady Clairol. She took a step back to take in the glorious sight of me, her youngest child, the apple of her eye, the joy of her soul. She clucked over my thinness, squeezed my arms, smooched my cheeks, ruffled my hair, and pulled me into the house. I caught sight of myself in the mirror that she had hung in her foyer. Dark red smudges of lipstick were left on both of my cheeks, and something glittery clung to my sweater. I looked down at my chest, and pulled away several stray sequins.

My mother has long been enamored with anything sparkly. Everyday, she wears a different top with sparkles and glitters. She routinely shops the clearance sales at Macy's for new sequined tops and costume jewelry. Decorative crystal hair combs are often stuck into her wild Israeli curls, and she uses more glitter hairgel and eye makeup than a high-school cheer squad. Today's sweater had several snowflakes knitted into the front, highlighted with silver sequins along the points of the flakes. Not to put too small a point on it, I can buy her any ugly piece of sparkling crap, throw it into a Swarovski bag, and she will declare me 'Son of the Year."

"Danny, sweetheart, are you hungry?" She asked. "You look hungry. You're so thin. Are you eating? You don't look like you're eating. Let me get you some soup. You'll love this soup." She bustled into the kitchen and came back out with a tray of food. "Sit down darling, sit down, eat some food. You want a sandwich? I'll make you a sandwich. You look so thin since that girl left you. Thank God, thank God" she briefly offered up, "she wasn't jewish, she never understood you. We'll get you a nice lunch and a nice jewish girl, and won't that be better?"

Right. That will fix everything—a nice jewish girl. "Um, Mom, I'm not really dating right now. I really need to get a job and get my life figured out before I get back out there."

"Nonsense! With today's shidduch crisis? There are way more single jewish girls than jewish boys, you can have your pick. Who cares that you don't have a job."

Um, single jewish women? I had no hope of hooking up, but no use fighting Mom. The shidduch crisis indeed. Jewish parents generally want their jewish children marrying other jews. The more religious of our faith will attempt to cement the transaction by engaging in a shidduch, or match. We're not talking about matchmaking in the sense of hard-core arranged marriages. We don't have thirteen year old girls getting married off, sight unseen, or anything sick like that. Today's shidduch is more like speed dating with intense family nosiness up-front. Young religious jews will hold off on dating through high school and career training until they think they are ready for marriage. Families will check out the credentials of potential spouses, making sure that family background, synagogue affiliation, and desired level of observance (post-marriage) are in alignment with both young people. The crisis arises due to the excess numbers of young jewish women who are interested in living religiously. Apparently, there are more observant orthodox women than men, and hence not enough religious jewish men for the jewish women to marry. I don't know whether my mother realizes it or not, but I'm not at all religious, so I factor in as a net cause of the shidduch crisis. Those pious religious girls would rather stay single than marry a sinner like me. And who are we kidding? I can't blame them. Putting myself back on the market won't help. Can't break it to Mom, so I might as well just pacify. "Ok mom, I'll think about it. Look mom, how are you doing?"

"Oh, you know, could be better. My back has been giving me so much trouble, and I have to go see the doctor about this bump that I found on my wrist. You never know with lumps and bumps..."

I zoned out comfortably, eating soup and sandwich while Mom went on and on about various minor ailments, real and imagined. Lunch was concluded with coffee, cookies, and a reiteration of my promise to get out on the town and find a sweet shayna maidel to bring home to my mama. Nineteen hugs and kisses later, and I was back on the street with a full stomach. I got into my car and surveyed the damage. Lipstick everywhere. I fruitlessly scrubbed at my cheeks with a couple of tissues before giving up. More sequins stuck in my sweater. Glitter was in my hair and stuck to my jeans. Who even knows where that came from. Well, since my washing machine had quit working this morning, it was going to stay there for a while—at least until I could find a Laundromat and determine whether I could afford to use it. My future shayna maidel had better be excited about glitter and home repair projects.

Mom can fuss and holler about her little baby needing a good lunch. I don't take her seriously all the time, but there may be something to her concern. Stuffed with her good cooking, I felt better prepared for hard knocks. I rolled back down the Orange line and strolled into DOES like I owned the joint. I sucked up stomach, puffed out my chest, made one more useless swipe at the lipstick smeared on my cheeks, and headed down to Pam's office.

"Danny!" Pam shrieked, "I don't BELIEVE it! Danny, please please please tell me that you made a job contact and are unemployed through no fault of your own?!"

"Pam, I made a job contact and I am unemployed through no fault of my own," I announced proudly.

"YES!" Pam screamed, pumping her fist in the air. "Yes! Yes! Yes!" She leapt up and ran around the desk, grabbing me in a bouncy hug. We hopped up and down together several times, shrieking "Yes! Yes! Yes!" I felt like I had just won the showcase showdown on The Price Is Right. We stopped bouncing, and I felt a little awkward.

"Hey Pam—why are we happy that I have no job?" I ventured.

"Danny, I think I've found a job for you. A real job. I just heard about it this morning. I called and asked a few questions, in case you were available. It's an office job, spreadsheet work, nice salary, good benefits. Even parking!" Pam crooned.

My heart sank. I'd applied to a hundred jobs that met that description in the past couple of months, all over the area and even the country, and none of the employers wanted me once they heard that my previous experience was with Almost Too Big To Fail. "Oh," I said weakly. "Great."

Pam must have seen the disappointment on my face. "Wait, Danny, don't get down. Keep the faith, my brother! I didn't tell you the best part. I *asked* them straight out, did they mind hiring former employees of Almost Too Big To Fail. Do you know what they said, Danny? Do you?" I shook my head. "Danny, not only did they say that they don't *mind* hiring folks from Almost Too Big To Fail, they WANT to hire from Almost Too Big To Fail! They think there were a few bad apples that are getting sorted out by the SEC, and a lot of good talent that hit the street when your old company shut down. They want to pick you up before someone else does!" Pam finished triumphantly.

A smile spread slowly across my face. "Pam, that's AWESOME!" I cried. "Tell me more!"

"Danny, just in case, I talked to them all about you specifically, on a no-name basis. If you are available, I can get you in there for an interview tomorrow morning. Here's the news I didn't give you—I'm not sure you're flexible for this." I braced myself for the worst. "The company is a lobbying firm. They lobby Congress for legislation that their clients are hoping to have passed. I know that's not everyone's cup of tea, but it's a job, right up your alley. Well? Are you up for it?"

I certainly was. Working for a lobbying firm wouldn't bother me at this point. I think I might go for it, even if it meant interviewing with Satan himself. Pam printed out a few copies of my resume and stuck them in a black vinyl portfolio. She phoned the company back and set up the interview. We concluded with several high fives and a little impromptu dancing and ass-bumping, then Pam hustled me out the door. "Go home, go home," she urged. "Make sure your interview suit is clean and your shirt is ironed. Check your tie for spots. Eat a good dinner. Get a good sleep. Your luck is going to change, Danny, I can feel it!"

I could feel it, too. I walked out into the soft glow of autumn sunset. The air was warm, mildly breezy, brushing over my cheeks. I felt perfectly happy. The smell of crisp leaves and fresh mown lawn drifted over from somewhere.

Back to the metro station. I trained back to Virginia, retrieved

my car from Metro parking, and headed home. I rolled into

the driveway and walked subdued into the house. My

confidence from DOES was beginning to subside. Anxiety

nagged at me. This job opportunity seemed too good to be true.

Why would they want me? What was the catch? I dwelt on

negativity for a while, then pushed my thoughts aside. Why

not think positive? I might end up with a real job, real money.

I could pay my bills, get out from under this house, and get a

better place to live. I could pay off the debt that I owed to my

company. I could pay my lawyer, Joe.

What the hell, time to call Joe. "Joe here," he answered.

"Hey man, it's Danny."

"Danny! What happened now?" Joe sounded panicked.

"Nothing bad," I cautioned. I have a good lead on a job interview tomorrow. Could be I'll be respectably employed this time tomorrow. I might be able to pay your bill after all."

"You're fucking with me," Joe laughed. "Really? That's great, man!"

"Yeah, well, hasn't happened yet, you know," I mumbled.

"Hey man, what's going on? Why so glum?" Joe asked. Then he started laughing. "Never mind. Shit, that wasn't kind. Why so glum *this* time?"

"Oh, you know, my mom is bugging me to find a nice jewish girl to settle down with. Like that's my priority right now."

"She picks now to get you out on the dating scene?"

"I know." I sighed. "No job, no money, and my house is falling to pieces. What a time to look for a lady, huh?"

Silence hung for a moment. Then Joe offered, "No job yet, but who knows how tomorrow will go? Think positive, don't be a downer. Maybe you *should* go out on a date."

I stared at the wall and wondered what the hell was going on with everyone in my life. "Look, you are so bummed out all the time, Danny. It would probably do you some good to get out there. You know, have some drinks, have a little fun. What could it hurt? Have a little dinner with a pretty lady. Have a good evening for once. Forget your troubles."

"That's an idea," I mused. "Just go have fun. I like it, I like it. I just don't know how to meet anyone."

"Hey, I have a few single lady friends. Someone might strike your fancy. What are you into?" Joe asked. *Tits and ass?* I thought.

"No!" I hissed to myself. "You pig! Guys don't really think like that, you're just doing what society has conditioned you to!"

"Come again?" asked Joe. *Shit,* I thought, *Danny, stop talking to yourself.*

"I don't know. This isn't really my idea. My mom wants me to find a nice jewish girl. You know. For the family."

"Wow, that's not just a stereotype then? What did she think when you married Lacey?" Joe asked interestedly.

"The usual. 'You're breaking my hea-art, Daaanny! How can you DOOOOO this to me, marrying outside the faith?' All at the same time she was munching down crab cakes. It was the most excellent case of hypocrisy I have ever viewed," I laughed.

"I have a good friend in mind for you, Danny. Let me give this good lady a call and set you up for Friday night. I'll text you the time and place. You show up, and be ready to have a nice evening with a classy lady."

Joe hopped off the call, and I put down the phone. Well, a date might not be a bad idea. If everything went well on

Thursday, I would have a job and maybe even a signing bonus to cover dinner. If not, I guess the enema car money would pay the bills. *Oh, negativity,* I thought, *just let it go.* The past few weeks and months would soon be just a drifting memory, a funny anecdote to chuckle over. *Hey, remember the time I lost my wife, my money, my job, and my house? Haha!* I changed into my flannel jammies and snuggled into bed. *This will be over soon,* I promised myself. *Just go to sleep now.* I tried to relax and drift off. Who know how long passed, when I sat upright in a panic. I fumbled for my cell phone and frantically checked to see if the alarm was set. It was—6:30 am, bright and early.

CHAPTER NINE

As it turned out, there was no need for the alarm. I jerked awake at 5:57 and couldn't get back to sleep. I got coffee going, then showered and shaved, and got into my gear. I slid right back into my morning groove, just like the good old days. Underclothes? Check. Shirt? Check. Pants? Check. Sock and shoes? Check. Stop for aftershave—slap slap—and comb the hair. Brush away all teeny tiny hairs that land on the shirt. Brush teeth and carefully spit so that nothing land on the shirt. Mouthwash. Tie? Check. Get that top button. Tighten the tie all the way up. Put on your suit jacket, sir— *you are a handsome devil*, I thought, looking at myself in the mirror. I looked good. Sharp. Professional. I grabbed the vinyl portfolio with my resume and headed out to the car, purposefully not focusing my eyes on the paint job.

I decided to park the car at the Metro station and train in to the interview, rather than risk having someone from the company see me in enema-mobile. Why not let that little surprise wait until after I locked down the job? I felt charged

up going through the fare gates with the other business people,

grabbing a copy of the free paper, squeezing into a full train,

heading downtown with the folks that know how to ride the

train. These were my people—they were dressed right, they

smelled right, and they were all checking devices for last

minute e-mails, reading reports, reading the paper, or zoning

into earbuds while playing Angry Bird. Exiting the station

was equally exhilarating—riding up the escalator, standing

firmly on the right, along with all of my fellow riders, while

leaving the full left side available for the energetic to charge on

up and get to work sooner. It was amazing to be back with my

people, leaving the station and standing on the corner with the

group waiting for the light to change, waiting for the DC police

to blow the whistles at cars that tried to run the red or block

the box. We hustled across the street together and sub-groups

peeled off the main group to enter into their respective office

buildings.

I followed a group of attractively dressed, older professional men into the lobby of my destination, and signed in at the security desk. Marble lined the floors, walls, and pillars of the lobby, and was accented with bright brass and crystal light fixtures. The lobby had a waiting area with Persian carpets, deep leather couches and glass tables, topped with fresh-cut flower arrangements. Sweet odor from the flowers drifted through the room. The security guard directed me to a bank of elevators around the corner. Seconds later, I was in a wood-paneled elevator rising silently up to the twelfth floor. The wood gleamed and I caught the lemony scent of furniture polish. Housekeeping in this building was several notches above what passed for housekeeping at my prior job. The elevator dinged and the doors opened right into the reception area for my job interview.

I had never been to a lobbying firm before, and wasn't sure what to expect. It certainly wasn't the bacchanalian excesses that general public opinion would have me believe.

The reception area was muted but elegant. Dark wood paneling covered the bottom third of the walls, and a palette of earth tones swept over the walls, couches, throw pillows. A couple of leather wing-back chairs and a low, mahogany coffee table completed the area. A side-bar held coffee mugs, a large coffee urn, sugar packets, milk jug, glasses, and a frosty glass urn of ice water with lemon slices layered in between ice cubes. A nattily-dressed, metrosexual male receptionist smiled at me. "Good morning," he greeted me. "May I help you?"

"Hello, I'm Daniel Rosenberg. I'm expected this morning—here for an interview?"

"Of course, Mr. Rosenberg. Please sign the register, and have a seat. I'll page Mr. Martin and let him know that you are here. Help yourself to some coffee or water, if you are interested."

I signed in and sat on one of the leather chairs. Several copies of the Wall Street Journal were carefully fanned out on the coffee table. The lead article was a scandalous expose on my former company. That wouldn't help me. I desperately

hoped that Pam was right, and that this company was

interested purely in talent, not in the random alignment of my

previous employment with the downfall of the national

economy.

"Mr. Rosenberg?" It was Mr. Martin. He was tall, dark

hair beginning to thin, and obviously got his five o'clock

shadow by three thirty every day. "Good to meet you." We

shook hands. "Come with me, and we'll get this started. Do

you want anything to drink first? Coffee? Tea? Water?"

I declined all drinks. No need to get me over-

caffeinated, who knows what I might say, and water may

result in a need to urinate in the middle of crucial interview

dialogue. "No thanks, I'm good. Thanks for the interview. I

read up on your company…" We chatted down the hallway,

and went into Mr. Martin's office.

Floor to ceiling windows opened to the east. I kept my

excitement inside. He had incredible views of the Capitol, the grayish-white mound back-lit by bright blue sky and clear morning light. "Nice office," I offered. He invited me to sit, and I pulled out a printer copy of my resume. Mr. Martin looked over it briefly, then handed it back to me. My smile stayed fixed, although I wasn't sure what to expect. Certainly not what came next.

"Well, Mr. Rosenberg. Should I call you Danny? Let me tell you how this is supposed to go. We really liked the sound of you from your DOES reference, and your resume backs up our instinct. It doesn't really matter to us that you worked for Almost Too Big To Fail. The SEC has rounded up anyone at your old company that had any true culpability, and as far as we're concerned, that means there's a lot of talent out on the street right now. Am I right?" He grinned broadly. I smiled back, a real smile this time. "Look Danny, this is almost a no-brainer, but we have to make the HR people happy. That means following the company's typical hiring procedures. We bypassed the phone interview, but we have to do a sit-down.

You'll be interviewing with four different people this morning. I'm the first. The other three will be folks that you would work with in the normal course of business. This is really more of a personality check than anything else. We're really excited to meet with you, and hope you'll consider our company as your new work home. Just relax, be yourself, and have fun getting to know the team."

This was great! Unbelievable. Absolutely what I needed. I couldn't believe there wasn't a catch. Wait—maybe they were going to low-ball me on the numbers. "So," I offered, "what do you need to know about me?"

"Well, Danny, we already know your skill-set, so why don't I just tell you about the job? It is of the utmost importance to our clients that we bring as much information as possible to the members of Congress when we present our proposals for future legislation. As one of our analysts, your core mission is to quantify the fiscal impact of the bills that our team will be presenting, using statistical modeling..." He continued on for a while, and then concluded, "along with a generous benefits package, which HR can tell you more about after hiring, and a starting salary of ..." He named a number in the low-to-mid unbelievables. Cripes, making money like that, I could catch up on my mortgage, buy a second home, buy a beach home, whatever! End of story. My life was about to change forever. "So, Danny, why don't we get you going on the round robin? And I'll see you again for lunch. Have a great morning!"

We shook hands again, and my next interviewer was at the door. She led me to her office, and we spent a pleasant twenty minutes complaining together about the local sports teams and discussing plans for the upcoming weekend. Our time must have concluded, because she wrapped up the chit-chat, handed me a business card, and escorted me to the next office. I thanked her and knocked on the door. The business man inside had his back turned to me, typing on his computer.

He gestured over his shoulder and invited me in. "Have a seat," he said, "Just finishing up an e-mail here."

I entered the office and took a seat in an upholstered chair in front of his desk. The desk and shelves were mahogany. A potted palm sat in the corner. Prints of landscape watercolors adorned the walls. Various corporate gifts sat on the book shelves and desk top, mixed in with paper files, financial magazines, and various books and journals on business and economics. Several framed family photos shared the credenza with the laptop that he was tapping into. Attempting small talk, I asked, "Is that your daughter? She's beautiful."

"Thank you!" the man said, still tapping. "Just about finished..."

I took a closer look at the photo. Beyond small talk, the girl really was beautiful, and strangely familiar. Where had I seen her before? Just then, the man swiveled around in his chair. "So, Mr. Rosenberg..." he said with a smile, before catching a look at my face. Just then, I realized where I had seen her before, and where I'd seen her father—last viewed from behind the humiliating Uncle Jimmy's visor. Dammit.

"You!" he hissed, his face frozen and his eyes darting around. I could tell that if we were not at his place of business, he would be manfully feeding me my own ass at this point. I was also frozen, not sure what to do. If I stayed, he would surely make my life hell, possibly call the police, and I would definitely not get the job. If I left, I would fail to complete the round robin interview, and I would definitely not get the job. What to do? My vote went with avoiding the police. I leapt out of my chair.

"Uh... sorry...wrong office... don't know who this Rosenberg is... supposed to interview but think I got placed in the wrong department," I improvised. "Um, this isn't catering, right?"

"You monster, you predator," he hissed, jumping out of his chair, "don't you move!"

Are you kidding me? I booked ass out of the office, and hustled my way down the hall. "Sorry, gotta go!" I said to the receptionist as I sailed by the desk, grabbing the register that I had signed on the way in. I pounded the elevator button and jumped into the next open lift, punching the Lobby button and sailing straight down. The guy didn't chase me onto the street, but I did get a voicemail on my phone letting me know that I didn't get the job. Of course I didn't. Of course.

Lobbying wasn't for me.

I moped on the train back home, then decided to put the day to good use, combing again through job offerings on the internet. It had to be just random bad luck for that guy to be at the lobbying firm. I wasn't destined to a life of unemployment and underemployment. If one sleazy company was willing to overlook my former employer, there must be dozens more out there that I just hadn't found yet. I identified four new job openings since my last crawl through the internet, and then stopped for a lunch break.

After a forgettable tuna sandwich, I drafted up custom cover letters for each job, then carefully cut and pasted the cover letters into e-mails, attached my resume to each one, then sent them off one by one. I updated my status on Facebook, fiddled away half an hour looking at my friends' status updates, and then went for a run. I made certain to bring my iPod along this time, music blasting and keeping all dangerous thoughts from entering my mind.

Friday brought more of the same. Looking for jobs, fiddling around on Facebook, eating, running. What a long, boring day. Joe had sent me a text message with the time and place for my dinner date with his friend, Deborah. I went through my grooming ritual all over again, but I really wasn't feeling it this time. It's not like I had a lot to offer this woman. I updated my Facebook status. "Going on a date. Wish me luck!"

I walked into the restaurant and headed to the bar to meet my date. This was my first encounter following my divorce, and I felt uncomfortable. I hadn't dated in years, not since just after college when Lacey and I were getting serious. I'd never been on a blind date before, and I wasn't sure how to present myself in the small talk kinds of questions. *What do you do?* Hmm. *I watch my life slowly erode into total shit...* probably not the most attractive approach.

I surveyed the bar. Most people sitting along it were already in couples. A few guys sitting solo. Not mine! Towards the end of the bar, a single lady. Dark hair, slender— she met the description. I walked up to her. "Excuse me, are you Deborah?" She turned and smiled.

"Danny? Nice to meet you," she said, extending her hand. Like her body, it was slender. Her palm was soft from lotion, and her nails were short but manicured. She was a picture of elegance—nicely styled hair, discreet diamond studs in her ears, a string of pearls at her neck. Tasteful makeup, a slight whisper of perfume, and casual business wear. Clearly, a successful lady at the end of her day. She had a glass of white wine in front of her already, which looked as though it had been partially sipped down, although there was no lip gloss mark on the wine glass.

"Nice to meet you too. That wine looks nice. Do you recommend it?" I asked. She did. I ordered a glass and turned towards her again. I wasn't sure what to say. What to do on a date? "L'Chaim," I offered, raising my glass.

"L'Chaim!" she said, clinking glasses with me, then lifting her glass. I watched for a moment, mesmerized, as she quickly flicked her tongue onto the lip of the glass, and then took a sip. No lipstick mark was left on the glass. I goggled at the move and small talk escaped me. Total cave man. Ugh, must talk. Cave man makes small talk. I nervously chugged down my wine and made my best stab. "So, Deborah, you work around here?" I tried.

"Yes, my firm is around the corner. How about you? You work around here? Joe didn't say what you do for a living."

"How do you know Joe?" I tried to redirect. Best to stay off the topic of my career. I chugged the rest of my wine. The bartender glanced at my glass and I quickly gestured for a refill. He tipped the bottle and deftly poured out another glassful, twisting the bottle with a flourish as he finished the pour.

"We went to law school together. Lots of fun—we survived the worst three years of our lives together, and stayed friends after. He hung out his own shingle, and I went into big law. How about you?" Why was she so interested in me? Couldn't she be just a little narcissistic? I really didn't want to talk about me. I chugged the wine again.

"Joe and I are buddies from college. He's a good guy. You know, he was worried I would be lonely after the divorce, so he offered to set me up." I set down my wine glass. That was good. No talk of work. My stomach felt warm. I started to feel relaxed and comfortable. Dating wasn't so hard. I could do this. I gestured for more wine.

"You're divorced?" Deborah looked a little off put.

"Yes, my wife just left me. The divorce just finalized. It started the string of the worst luck in my life." *Shut up, Danny. She looks pissed. Change the topic.* I couldn't. I chugged more wine, hoping it would stop me, but the words started to bubble out, vomiting out the horror of my life. "She took me for everything, and then the housing market dumped. So I'm sitting on an upside-down mortgage on my house, which is falling apart. I can't afford to maintain it, much less fix it. I worked for Almost Too Big To Fail. Then I lost my job, and I can't find a new one, so I'll probably lose the house altogether. I live each day in fear that I'll be subpoenaed for the SEC investigation. I've applied for jobs everywhere and the only place that hired me is Uncle Jimmy's." *Little white lie. That's okay. You can tell her the rest when you're further into the relationship.* "Even they fired me." *But no need to say why.* "I don't know what I'm going to do." Deborah took this all in with an expression that was initially hostile, then bored, then mildly amused. Now she laughed. "I could end up on street

corner. I don't know why I'm telling you all of this. I haven't

even told my mother all of this. You're just so easy to talk to."

I smiled and leaned my head on my elbow, which slipped a

little on the shiny wood of the bar. My head dropped abruptly.

I quickly propped myself back up again. "You're so pretty.

This is great. You seem like you really have your life together.

I used to be on the up and up. I have a Masters' degree, and a

Beemer. I just don't know what's happened to my life."

Deborah smiled, and leaned forward towards me. Oh,

God, she was ok with all of this. Unbelievable. She wasn't

pissed. Maybe she knew how tough times were. Maybe she

didn't care that I didn't have a thing. Maybe big-law paid her

enough money that she didn't mind picking up the tab for

dinner. God, I hoped so. She smelled great. She leaned right

up and put her lips next to my ear. My lips parted and the

slightest drop of drool rolled out the corner of my mouth. I was

mesmerized. She cooed into my ear. "Danny?"

"Yeah..."

Her glossy lips were right outside of my ear canal. I could feel her sweet warm breath tickle right into my brain. I started to feel an erection forming. I strained to hear her delicate whisper. "I just put fifty dollars on the bar. I'm going to get up and go to the ladies room now..."

"Okay," I agreed eagerly.

"When I get back..."

"Yes?"

"I'm really hoping that you'll be gone. Because if you aren't, I'm going to have to find a different place for dinner." She hopped off the bar stool and patted my arm. "Best of luck, buddy. Just don't ever do this on a first date again." I stared at her perfect ass in amazement as she sashayed off to the ladies' room, then banged my head down on the bar.

It couldn't get more clear than that. Morosely, I made my way back home, where I ate leftover tuna fish for dinner. I got back onto the laptop and noticed a slew of folks had commented on my status. Good luck. What a lucky lady. Have a great dinner. One from Lacey! "I'm so proud of you, Danny. You're finally moving on!"

When we got divorced, Lacey and I didn't UnFriend each other on Facebook, but we had also maintained a policy of silence. I had no idea that she was watching my page or cared what I was doing. Maybe I should check her out, too. I hovered the cursor over her name and clicked into her profile, and started looking over all of the details of her new life. Lacey is in a relationship. Lacey studied at some art institute. Lacey lived in Ecovillage Ashram. Lacey worked in Ecovillage Ashram. What was that? Lacey's profile picture was just her face. She was smiling and looked happy. Her status read, "Our website is finally up! Check us out!" and had a link to the website for Ecovillage Ashram.

I started to feel a little uncomfortable. Was I prying? Was I stalking? I rationalized with myself that it was okay to look at the information that Lacey had posted on the internet. That was the point, right? If she wanted to keep her information private, she wouldn't have put it out there for the world to see, right? I clicked into the website for Ecovillage Ashram. The home page of the website showed a cultivated green field rolling up into a hill, where a few hobbit-like houses clustered into the hillside. Trees backed the houses. At the bottom of the picture, a menu offered links to About Us, FAQs, How To Visit, Gift Shop, Photos, Lacey's Blog, and Contact Us.

I clicked on Photos. A page came up and began a slideshow of images, starting with the photo from the homepage. The photos that slid through showed a happy looking group of people tending the plants in the field, building the hobbit houses, doing outdoor yoga, painting at easels, working at a pottery wheel. Lacey's happy, pretty face was sprinkled throughout the pictures. Lacey with muddy hands, bowed intently over a potter's wheel, forming a bowl. Lacey, holding up freshly picked vegetables and grinning broadly.

Lacey, stretched long and serious, her head tipped back and her foot pulled up hard in a yoga pose. Lacey, stuck in the middle of a group of ladies, all of them smiling and posing. Lacey, kissing one of the ladies. WHOA! I scrolled down and clicked on About Us.

> Founded by Lacey Miller and inspired by her vision of feminist self-expression, Ecovillage Ashram is a womyn-only intentional community in the heart of Tennessee, where we embrace a lesbian lifestyle grounded in ecology, veganism, self-expression, and feminine love. We believe life is art and encourage all people to richly weave the tapestry of their lives. We reject patriarchy and further reject its inverse, matriarchy, including reproduction. All participants in Ecovillage Ashram share the vision that no creature, be it animal or person, should be indentured in the involuntary servitude of people. We believe that the womyn's body is most free when it sustains only its own life, and remains uncontaminated by foreign life-sources that seek to enslave and subjugate a womyn into lifesupport for parasitical growth. We participate daily in spiritually enlightening group yoga sessions, strengthening both body and soul.
>
> Here at Ecovillage Ashram, we also believe in reducing our environmental footprint to the barest trace of toes and heel. Our homes are designed and self-constructed to have as little environmental impact as possible. All electricity is generated by solar panels and interior construction is completed using a blend of locally-gathered materials and the most advanced green

products on the commercial market. We create no trash, as all excess materials are composted or recycled.

Further, at Ecovillage Ashram we reject the artificial economic inequality created by a capitalist society. We cooperatively farm our own organic foods. The members of our community freely share their skills and abilities with each other, operating in a cash-free, mutually beneficial manner. However, in order to maintain cashflow to support the acquisition of construction materials and additional land for future expansion, we sell selections of our objects of art in the gift shop to external visitors. As group artists, no one participant receives individual credit for the creation of the objects of art, and the proceeds benefit the community as a whole.

Spontaneous, nonbinding, mutually consensual romantic expression is welcomed and encouraged. All are free to share their love. Free expression creates joy, which furthers the artistic capacities of all who share. Love inspires much of the tangible art produced at Ecovillage Ashram.

Ecovillage Ashram welcomes visitors throughout the year, and is currently soliciting new potential participants, particularly those with background in construction, plumbing, chiropractic healing, and homeopathic arts.

Whoa. Sounded like there was a lot that Lacey hadn't

shared with me when we were married. For one thing, that

she wanted to go back to her maiden name. I clicked on

"Lacey's Blog." Maybe that would illuminate why she had

decided to leave me and our comfortable lives for a radical

lesbian commune. Was I really so awful to live with? The blog

loaded up with an entry from two days ago on the community

harvest festival. A picture of Lacey and some of her friends

was in the middle of the entry. They were all happy and

sweaty, looking tan and relaxed, standing on the edge of a field

in the middle of baskets full of squash. On the sidebar there

was a menu with archived entries back to 2006. *That's*

strange, I mused. Lacey and I had gotten married in 2005, and

she never mentioned having a blog while we were married. I

clicked into the archive and selected one of the older entries. It

read like a journal:

> Another hard day today. Another early miscarriage.
> This is the third one in six months. Danny still hasn't
> noticed that I'm not on the pill, that I keep having tired
> weeks and late periods. I left work today when the
> spotting started, and went straight to the doctor's office.
> No heartbeat, no fetal pole. Just an empty gestational
> sac. She gave me a prescription for Cytotec, and I came
> home to cramp and bleed. Danny called a while ago and
> said he would be home late. Boys' night out! I need to
> get my own hobbies. There doesn't seem to be much
> point in waiting for Danny to care about our futures,
> keep me company, or be interested in what I want to do.

My doctor offered to write a referral for me to visit the fertility clinic, to see if there is a medical reason for all of these miscarriages. I think I'll pass. I wanted to have a baby to have a normal marriage, but what is the point if I'm already married to a baby? I need to find a way to live for myself, instead of living for the people around me. After all, who is going to live for me, if I don't live for myself?

Oh my God. No wonder she left me. I was a total asshole! I had no idea that my ex-wife had multiple miscarriages over the course of our short marriage. Had I been that checked out? Was I really that unavailable to her?

I spent the rest of the weekend reading through Lacey's blog archives, getting to know the woman that I had been married to. The pottery had become her hobby, and then her passion, and then she had several affairs with other women before finally leaving me. She used the money from the divorce to buy a large piece of land in Tennessee where she and her friends founded an intentional community. In between discovering who my ex-wife was, I puttered around the house, and waited for Monday to come. Maybe on Monday would come a new job opportunity. Maybe Monday would

bring redemption.

CHAPTER TEN

Monday morning finally arrived, and I headed back out to DOES. I slowly walked through the door and down the hall, poking my head into Pam's office. She was on the phone, but quickly ended her call when she saw my face.

"Oh Danny," said Pam. "Danny, Danny, Danny. What are we going to do with you? I thought this last job was right up your alley. What happened?"

"Um, the guy knew me," I said. "When I was working for Uncle Jimmy's, I delivered a pizza to his house seven minutes late. I never had a chance." It was a good lie. Why not extend it a little? No need to bother Pam with my unintended underage faux pas.

"Danny, we're really scraping the bottom of the barrel here for you. I've never seen someone get started with so many jobs just to have them turn out bad. I'm going to have your next check approved, but let's really get you working just for the day at least. Here's a guy. He just called today, he wants help tomorrow morning unloading off his boat. Sounds like maybe he's a fisherman. Who knows, if you do a good job, you could get something regular going in the mornings. Why don't you give it a try?"

I thanked Pam and went on my way, putting the reference slip in my pocket. I went home and went to sleep, sleeping hard all night long. I didn't wake at all or even dream—suppose my brain had decided that enough was enough. Time to check out, get some rest, and wait until the morning to see what new hell awaited and where DOES would send me.

DOES sent me down to the Washington DC waterfront. My next job opportunity was just temporary, unloading cargo from a boat for the morning. I wandered around the boat slips, looking for the Mickey D.

The Mickey D was a battered-looking boat, splattered with rust spots. Boat leprosy. "Knock knock!" I called out hopefully. A tired-looking man with wiry, graying red hair stepped out of the cabin, and wandered my way. "Hi, sir, Danny Rosenberg, DOES sent me out to help you for the morning. Unloading? Are we unloading fish today?" I asked.

He dredged up phlegm from the back of his throat and spat out into the water, then stared silently out across the river long enough for me to get really uncomfortable. "Fish," he harrumphed. "No fucking fish." He turned and went back into the cabin. I wasn't sure what to do. I stood for a minute or two, then decided to get on the boat. I made my way to the cabin, and poked my head in. The stale scents of whiskey and vomit, lamp oil and gunpowder layered over each other, along with the smell of the holocaust deaths of millions of cigarettes. Battered and scratched wood-panel walls were mounted with oil-lamps and hung with fading pictures of men in army uniforms—buddies with arms around each other, guys standing with guns, guys poking heads out of tanks, guys in tents, stiff-faced formal poses in dress uniform. Some of the pictures clearly depicted a younger Ronald. Guns in various stages of disassembly were strewn around the cabin. Bullets and shells were randomly scattered on a scarred Formica table and spilled onto the floor. A couple of buckets in the corner held bent and twisted lumps of lead. A small TV with a built-in VCR sat in the corner on the floor, with a few stacks of video tapes next to it. A brief glance at the videotape cases showed Ghostbusters, Indiana Jones, E.T., a few pornos, the Rise and Fall of the Third Reich. Ok, so Ronald was a fan of the classics. I pulled my head out of the cabin swiftly, shook it back and forth for a moment, took a deep breath, and steeled myself to try going in again.

"Um, sir? Hi. I didn't get your name. I mean, in my mind you look like a Ronald, but I don't want to call you Ronald. I mean, if it's not your name," I babbled, "so maybe you'll..." I trailed off as he turned and gave me a hard, angry look. He banged his fist into the wood paneling, causing an oil-lamp to briefly bounce from its wall mounting before clinking back against the wood.

"You need to just shut the hell up, penis breath," he snarled out. "I've got one hell of a hangover and no fucking fish. This is a houseboat, not a fucking fishing boat. I've gotta unload a lot of crates, you donkey-dick mother fucker, and you are here to help me. Silently."

Whoa. Noted. I guess I'd have to call him Ronald if he wouldn't offer up his real name. Ronald was in desperate need for some anger management classes and possibly a stint in rehab. I stood silently and waited for him to tell me what to do. He scratched, yawned, and motioned me out of the cabin and down to the cargo hold. He grunted at me, gesturing for me to open it. I did, and stared down at the crates below. "Is that guns?" I gasped. "You're a gun runner?"

"Are you stupid or just fucking retarded?" he roared at me. "That's military surplus MREs. Not guns. I have to get those off the ship and onto my truck. Start pulling those up out of the hold. And stop talking."

Not the most social job I'd ever had. I started humping the crates up out of the hold and stacking them on the deck, where Ronald picked them up and loaded them into the back of his truck. "Don't lift with your fucking back," Ronald MacDonald yelled. "Lift with your legs, anus."

Jeez, he really knew how to curse. I don't know that I'd ever heard any one curse so much. I got most of the MREs hauled up from the hold, and looked around to see what else there was to do. Ronald decided that he was on break, and cracked open a bottle. I sneaked a peek out of the corner of my eye, and saw him belting down a slug of Rebel Yell whiskey at 9:37 in the morning. Holy crap. He was angry enough sober. I wondered how mean he would get if he was loaded. I went back down into the hold. Maybe he would forget about me.

A few minutes later Ronald was clearly in a much better mood. "Smoke break!" he hollered. "Princess, get your ass up here."

I climbed out of the cargo hold. Ronald was cheering up, now that the booze was working its way through his system. "Um, can I go to the bathroom?" I asked.

"Eh, just take a piss off the side of the boat," he offered generously. "If you gotta take a shit, go to the head. Here, have a fucking cigarette." He thrust a lit cigarette into my hand. Not knowing what to do, I wandered back and pulled open the door to the head. An unbelievable mess lay before me. The walls were brown. The seat was brown. The floor... was brown. I recoiled.

"Um... Is there any..." I began, before just stopping. I couldn't ask Ronald for cleaning supplies. He'd kick my ass and call me "Nancy." Oh well. I tried the next door. Maybe it would be a supply closet with mops and Lysol. Maybe Ronald was well-stocked with Soft Scrub, all evidence thus far to the contrary. As I pulled open the door, a pungent odor drifted out. I sighed. I was so tired of all of the pungent odors on this boat. Wait a minute... this pungent odor was familiar, reminiscent of my college days. My eyes widened as I realized that the closet was packed full of bales of marijuana. Holy shit! I tossed the cigarette aside and reached a hand out to touch the shrink-wrapped green goodness. I wondered if there was any way I could get paid part in cash and part in greenery. Ronald roared from the front of the boat, and I jerked my hand back and stepped back, ready to deny any intentions of touching. I turned, and saw in horror that a fire had broken out in the front cabin. The cabin full of wood—and lamp oil— and bullets.

"RONALD!" I screamed. "RONALD! DO YOU HAVE ANY FIRE EXTINGUISHERS?"

"GET THE FUCK OFF THE BOAT, ASSHOLE!" he retorted. I ran to the back and jumped into the water, swimming furiously around the next boat, ducking at the sounds of the bullets exploding in the fire. Sirens screamed and several fire trucks pulled up. I tread water, waiting to be rescued. Was this my fault? Had the cigarette that I tossed caught the cabin on fire? I was pulled out of the water by fire men on a fireboat, and watched in amazement as the burnt-out shell of the boat tipped and slowly sank into the water. Ronald stood on the dock, smoking silently, staring at what remained of the Mickey D. I approached him slowly.

"Ronald...sir? I'm sorry. I don't know what happened. I..." I trailed off.

"Shut the fuck up, princess," he snapped. "I'll talk to you after the fire marshall leaves. Now you go to the truck and wait for me." As instructed, I walked to the truck. The back was loaded up with the crates of the MREs. I felt guilty as hell and scared shitless. I had burned down this man's home. He had nothing left in the world but a crappy truck and a bunch of MREs, and it was all my fault. I wouldn't be surprised if he drove me out into the woods and hacked me to pieces.

Ronald spent a few more minutes with the fire marshall. He signed some papers, shook the guy's hand, and then walked my way.

"Alright, penis-breath, let's go get a drink," he said. He climbed in and started up the truck.

"Hey, Ronald...I...Look, can you tell me what your name really is? I can't keep calling you Ronald," I said.

"You dumb fuck, that is my name. Ronald. Red fucking hair, everyone has called me Ronald MacDonald my whole life. That's why me and my army buddy named the boat the Mickey D."

What a surprise! Who knew. I'd gotten his name right all morning. "Oh, the boat, sir, I'm so sorry about the boat. So sorry. I think that cigarette I threw might have caught it on fire."

He snorted. "Gimme a fucking break. Yeah, I told the fire marshall that you didn't know what to do with the fucking cigarette, and how I wanted to shove it up your ass for burning down my boat. He thought you looked like a dipshit, too, and wrote it down as an accidental fire. Ronald cackled, and fear rippled through me. "I had just doused the cabin with lamp oil and set it on fire myself. Promised my buddy I would. Buried him yesterday, put the boat down today. Piece of shit. He had it insured for a hell of a lot, though, and he named me beneficiary on the policy. I'm rich as hell now. Good guy, took care of his buddy. Let's go drinking."

This reminded me that Ronald had already been drinking. He pulled up to a liquor store, and came back out with a case of bottles. The bottles went in the back of the truck with the MREs, and Ronald and I took off on a bender.

CHAPTER ELEVEN

Wednesday morning, I woke up with a start. I was cold and cramped, and my face was stuck to something hard, cold and scratchy. After a moment, I realized that it was grass. I sat up a little and a wave of nausea hit me. I leaned over and vomited into the gutter.

That was it. Officially, I was a bum. I had gotten drunk with some random maniac, passed out, and slept the night on a random curbstrip. Add public vomiting to my list of crimes. My mother would be ashamed. I was ashamed. "Amigo!" someone cried out. A chorus rose up. "Amigo! Amigo!" One voice called out, "Demasiada cerveza!" Too much beer. I vomited again. "Demasiada tequila, tambien," someone added.

Too much beer is right, I thought to myself. God, where the hell was I? I looked around and realized that I was at a shopping center on Little River Turnpike, right in front of the Safeway.

Around me were a number of guys, standing on the frozen grass, dressed in paint-stained or work-grimy clothes. They clustered in groups, talking, staring silently into traffic, or just zoning out. A few of them were looking at me, laughing, and then talking amongst themselves. They hustled up to me and hauled me up to my feet, laughing and brushing pieces of dead grass off of me.

"Demasiada cerveza, amigo!"

"Necessitas ayuda?"

"Digame, digame—una muchacha, verdad?"

As they helped me up good-naturedly, speculating on how and why I was in this condition, I swooned a little then stood on my own. My head was foggy and it felt like a spike was pounding its way into the left half of my cranium. My mouth tasted like vomit and I desperately needed to pee. Unfortunately, just then a large van pulled up onto the access road and a beefy-looking guy hopped out of the passenger side.

His bushy, reddish-gold hair burst out in a short pony-tail from the back of his beat-up ball cap. A bristling beard and mustache combination covered most of his face. What was left to be seen was sweaty, pinky-red skin and tiny, crinkled dark eyes. "Hey, I need five guys today, okay? Cinco muchachos, hurry up now. You, you, you, you, you!" He hollered, pointing at me and the guys around me. One of the guys started to speak up in protest, surely to point out that I had no business getting hired for the day.

"Hey, shut up!" said the sweaty guy. "Get in the fucking truck right now or I'll start picking up guys at Home Depot from now on!"

That was it. My new buddies hauled me onto the truck. A new wave of nausea clenched in my stomach and I tried not to hurl. The beefy guy swung the back of the van closed, and I groaned. I get carsick any time I have to ride in a backseat, and this van didn't have seats, seatbelts, or even windows back in the cargo area where we were now squatting.

The van lurched through traffic, starting and stopping. I belched and held my hand over my mouth, desperate not to throw up. Beefy red-neck would undoubtedly kick my ass if I sullied his truck. My guys quickly conferred and then a couple of them shoved plastic, 7-11 bags my way. One contained a couple of donuts. Another had two large plastic bottles— lemon-lime Gatorade and Coca-cola. I gorged on the food and drink, and the nausea subsided along with the headache. My need to pee, however, grew worse and worse. The van kept going and going. "Hey guys," I whispered, "when do we get there? I need to pee."

"Hey, shut the fuck up!" hollered beefy redneck. One of my new friends put his finger to his lips in a shushing gesture. Clearly these guys had worked for beefy redneck before. He grabbed my empty Gatorade bottle and gestured with it. I closed my eyes, and rested my head against the side of the van. Obviously, it was going to be a long, long ride, or else my amigo would never suggest that I make a trucker bomb. Every time I think my life is at its new low, Fortune comes along to prove that it can always get worse.

I quietly shuffled my way back to the very far back of the cargo area, as far from beefy redneck as I could get. I turned my back, uncapped the bottle, unzipped, and aimed. I filled the bottle and forced myself to stop—not fun. I think I could have peed all day. I recapped the bottle. Not knowing what else to do with it, I put it back in the 7-11 bag. I closed up my pants and closed my eyes again. I didn't want to make eye contact with anyone for a while.

Eventually the van pulled to a stop. Beefy redneck stomped around to the back and pulled open the cargo door. I stepped out into the morning, and my eyes focused on the enormous yard before us. This was definitely more than a five-man job. Just behind the van was a larger panel truck. The other guys were swarming around to the back of it, and unloading lawn care equipment—a lawn mower, edger, leaf blower, etc. I made a move to go to the truck also.

"You," hollered beefy redneck. "You speak English? Go in the back, start pulling out the weeds around the bushes. Your friends already took all the machines, I need some handwork done. Take your shit with you now," he warned as I began to walk off. I stepped back and pulled my special 7-11 bag out of the back of the van. What to do with it? Could I pour it out? Would it ruin the grass? I guess I'd watch for trash cans on the property and try to dispose of it. I pulled some gloves and lawn bags out of the back of the panel truck.

The front yard alone was easily a half-acre. I began walking, not sure what I was really supposed to do in the back yard. I guess I'd just find the bushes and pull out any plant that didn't look pretty. God knows why I was doing this, but I was pretty certain that if I didn't work the day through, I wouldn't have a ride back to the Safeway, and I had no idea where I was, no money, and no cell phone. Better just to get exploited for a few hours, and possibly paid, than to walk who knows how far to get home.

The backyard had a huge, multi-story wooden deck protruding from the rear of the house. The bottom level of the deck led out onto a flag-stone patio with an outdoor fireplace. More flag-stones led out on a path to a huge whirl-pool hot tub, pouring over a waterfall into a sparkling blue swimming pool. Beyond the pool was a wide expanse of grass lawn, fully encircled by bushes. Ivy hugged around the base of the bushes, and climbed up the hill, where the landscaping blended into a wooded area.

The owners of this house had really spent time and money making the yard look beautiful. I guess that's where me and my crew came in. We were supposed to keep it all groomed. I snapped open a black plastic lawn bag, pulled on some gloves, and wandered into the bushes. It looked like earlier in the year, the ivy had done an effective job as ground-cover, keeping out most weeds under the bushes, but in the cool weather, the ivy leaves were changing color. They looked really pretty, but weeds were beginning to poke out from the vines, and many of the weeds were too small to pull with my gloves on. I pulled off my gloves, and began to yank out the weeds, stuffing them into the black lawn bag.

The size of the yard was incredible. I pulled weeds for hours, while my cohorts trimmed the lawn, edged around the flagstones, and blew away trimmings. My back was killing me from hauling the MREs the day before, and my headache returned as I sweated. I was incredibly thirsty, had random dizzy spells, and began to worry about passing out. I was trying to figure out how I had arrived at this place. Random flashes came back to me over the course of the morning. The fire. Jumping from the boat. As I sweated, the smell that radiated off of my body was horrific—the pungent stench of clothes that had soaked in the Potomac river, dried on my body, slightly mildewed, and now dampened again from the sweat. I hadn't had a shower in over twenty four hours. More memories flashed back in my mind. Sitting in Ronald's battered, rusty truck, bouncing around on the cheap, cracked vinyl pleather seat, held together with duct tape. Fearing for my life. Drinking cheap whiskey with Ronald. My palms began to blister from pulling weeds. I struggled to recall how I had ended up at the Safeway, trying to connect the memory dots. Ronald talking to me. "Hey dumbfuck, if you can't afford an electrician, go pick up some fucking wetbacks. They're almost free, they work so cheap. I won't hire those fuckers, I pay my fucking taxes. But you've gotta do what you've gotta do!" Shit, Ronald had dropped me off there so that I could hire someone to fix up my house. What a misfire. End result was me, slaving away to beautify some deep South plantation home. Finally beefy redneck came around and told us to take a lunch break. We all sat down on the flagstones. I had no food. My amigos split up what was in their 7-11 bags and ate. I pulled my bag out, then remembered what was in it, and set it back down. I idly scratched my arms.

Looking down, I realized that the bushes must have thorns on them—there were red scratches up and down both arms. My amigos gradually stopped chatting with each other and stared collectively at my arms in horror. I scratched a little more, then stopped. My arms were developing blisters like those on my palms, and my fingers were puffing up. Everything hurt. Bemused, I just stared. The guys jumped up and began hollering in Spanish. One grabbed my 7-11 bag. I felt funny and dizzy, disconnected with reality, as he pulled out the Gatorade bottle, twisted it open, and began sloshing the contents all over my arms. A part of my brain tried to alert me that I was being doused with my own urine, but not soon enough. My throat got tight, my breath was constricted. I was suffocating. Everything went dark.

When I woke up, sirens were blaring and beefy redneck was talking. "Yeah, picked these guys up to do some work today. No, don't know his name. No, no insurance. Didn't tell me his name. Just started working and got into the fucking poison ivy. Must be allergic. Dumb shit. Lucky his amigo had an epi-pen. Otherwise he'd be dead. Yep, you can take him, that's all I've got."

The paramedics loaded me onto a gurney and into the ambulance. I was taken to the hospital and evaluated. All of my clothes except my jacket were thrown away and I was rubbed all over with alcohol swabs and ointments. The nurse gave me scrubs to wear so that I wouldn't have to go home in a bare-ass hospital gown. I was also given prescriptions for topical ointment and an epi-pen, and discharged with strict instructions to stay the hell away from poison ivy. "Don't forget to swing by the finance office on your way out," mentioned the nurse.

Paperwork in the finance office wasn't fun. I was out of work and have no insurance. "Will this be self pay?" asked the cashier. "Cash, check or credit card?"

"How much is the bill?" I asked.

"One thousand, six hundred and twenty two," she responded.

"WHAT!" I shouted. "I've been here for eighty two minutes! How could it cost so much? Is that the ambulance?"

"No, the ambulance is billed separately. That company provides an independent service. This bill is just for the hospital services." She replied.

"Is it the doctors? Elitist bastards," I frothed.

"Oh, no the doctors also each bill separately."

I frantically thought back on who had seen me during my stay. Cripes, it was at least three doctors. "So I could be looking at thousands here? And I have to pay it all myself? I'm out of work. Doesn't Obamacare cover any of this? What was the good of sending the country into socialized medicine and running up the deficit if I still have to pay my own hospital bills? Our country has been screwed by the politicians. I can't believe this," I ranted on. The clerk nodded sympathetically.

"Don't I know it, hon, it's a darn shame what those Democrats have done to us. They're betrayed the founding fathers' vision and sold this country out to the communists. Next thing you know, we'll be eating rice and speaking Chinese. If you want, you can come to my political meeting next week and help out to make real change," she offered, handing me a pamphlet. I glanced at the pamphlet and saw it was promotional materials for the John Birch Society. Cringe. I stuffed it into my pocket and plunged ahead.

"Um, I'll think about it, thanks for the offer. I think I've got plans already, though. Can we just set up a payment plan for me?" I urged. Ten minutes later, I was out the door.

Poison ivy. How the hell was I supposed to know that was poison ivy? I had never mown a lawn in my life. Plants were mysterious green things that other people took care of. Fruits and vegetables came from the grocery store, and preferably came out of cans and jars. I collapsed on a bench outside of the hospital. My hands slipped into my pockets. I found a thick piece of paper in one pocket, and pulled it out. An envelope. On the back was writing, in two different ink colors and two different handwritings. One, in blue ink and crabbed lettering, said, "Thanks for the help, man. You passed out before I could pay you. You are one crazy mother fucker! Ronald." The other, in black ink and round letters, said, "4.5 hours x $10 hour = $45. Stay out of the poison ivy, dipshit." Inside the envelope was $85.

I had no ride home, and my car was still parked at the Metro station parking lot from two days ago. I wandered back in, asked to use the finance clerk's telephone, and called a cab. She took the time to press several more pamphlets on me, and I thanked her, surreptitiously tossing them into a trash can as I walked back out of the hospital to wait for the cab. It pulled up about ten minutes later, and the driver whisked me off towards the Metro station to get my car.

"Hey man, how are you," I offered. "How do you like driving a cab?"

"Great, great," he said. "I make good money. My house will be paid off in three more years. I'm saving for my kids' college. And I'm always time in home to pick my kids up from school. It's flexible, you know? I worked in an office for years, but my wife got sick of it. I do this now, and she's much happier. Happy wife, happy life." He chuckled. I wondered how people would feel about riding in a BMW cab with enema bags painted on the outside, and then shook the thought aside. Better to leave that one for Pam to suggest. The cab pulled up at the Metro station, and I paid the driver and tipped him $10. "Wow, thank you!" he said.

"Take care of those kids," I said. I headed into the house and collapsed on my couch.

CHAPTER TWELVE

I spend the rest of Wednesday and most of Thursday recovering from my bender and poison ivy drama. I had a hell of a rash, but the doctors had assured me that I wouldn't spread the infection to others. I still got lots of funny looks when I went to the drugstore to fill my prescriptions, so I also bought a box of gloves. I guess if anyone was really nervous, I could wear the gloves to avoid skin-to-skin contact.

By Thursday afternoon I felt sufficiently recovered to head back to DOES. I only had one job contact for the week, and needed another if I was going to get my unemployment check. Pam wasn't surprised to see my, since my job with Ronald had just been a day job. "Hey Danny, what took you? I thought I'd see you yesterday morning. Busy?"

"Oh yeah," I mumbled, "decided to do a little yardwork and got into a little poison ivy."

"Stay back," Pam hollered, "I hate that stuff. Don't touch anything in my office. I am so allergic it doesn't even matter."

"No problem, I'll just stay here, just wanted to see if you have anything for me."

Pam punched the keys in her computer. "I don't know, Danny. I don't think I have much for you. All I have here is IT stuff. Do you have any computer skills? Any certifications that you're holding out on me?"

I cleared my throat and shuffled my feet. "no."

"What was that?" Pam asked. I looked up.

"No. I have no skills. Nothing that will help me get an IT job. Nothing that will help me get any job." I hung my head, and turned slightly aside. I swallowed hard. I stared at her wall of family members. Happy people who had passed through this office, found a job, made their way. Those people had regained their pride. They knew who they were and what they were doing. That wasn't me. I was out of the loop, unemployable. I was low. I was nothing.

Pam stared at me, then got up and walked around her desk. She came right up to me and pushed her finger into my chest. HARD. I stared down at her stubby finger, the acrylic nails polished dark red with gold palm trees overlaid on the manicure. Her skin was dark brown and her knuckles were slightly ashy. "WHO are YOU?" she barked. "WHO THE HELL ARE YOU?" I stared at here, stammering slightly then falling silent. "YOU are NOT Danny Rosenberg. The Danny I know has pride. He has stamina. He is not a quitter! He's a tryer! Now WHO ARE YOU!? Are you DANNY? Or are you some SORRY ASSHOLE THAT NEEDS TO GET OUT OF MY OFFICE! Because if you're just some SORRY ASSHOLE, I'll give you a coffee mug to shake on the corner. You can beg for loose change and sleep on a bench. I'll call some people, they'll bring you cocoa at midnight and you can line up in the park to get your breakfast on holidays. But if you are DANNY, I'll give you a job referral and you can try like a man to have a job and earn back some self respect!"

"I'm Danny," I said quickly. "I'm Danny. I'll give it a try. I'm sorry, Pam."

Pam smiled. "You don't have to be sorry, honey. You just hang in there." She hugged me, and handed me a referral slip. "Now good luck with this. I'll give them a call and let them know you're coming. Have a great weekend, too!"

The job was with Metro-Hi-Tek, some small, local IT company that offered e-mail services. It had been common ten or fifteen years ago to find these small local companies, offering relatively cheap dial-up service, but now nearly all IT services were through cable or phone companies, high-speed broadband lines. I wondered how MetroHiTek was hanging in there with such heavy competition. The job was for the night shift. I showed up at the address, and met the night shift manager, Jeff. He was in casual clothes and had a bunch of fast food bags spread out in front of him. He also seemed to be the only guy around.

"This job is really easy, it's help desk. All you have to do is answer the phone, see what problem the person is having, and check the binder for the solution. Usually the solution is easy—like turn off your computer and turn it back on. That solves about 90 percent of user problems. Other problems can be solved by making sure the computer is plugged in, the battery is functional, resetting the password, and so forth. If you aren't able to find a five-minute solution in the binder, you open up a trouble ticket and get it in the queue. The network administrators address issues in the queue based on priority. Usually first in line gets priority, but sometimes issues can be elevated depending on the importance of the user, the importance of the data they are trying to access, or the importance of whatever failure is keeping the user from the data. Any questions so far?"

"Yeah, if its so easy, then why doesn't everyone take this job?"

"Ha! Good question. Well, help desk is the lowest of the low for IT. The pay is crappy and the hours are worse. There's lots of night shift and weekend work, because help desk is needed 24/7. So qualified personnel are hard to find—usually, they work help desk for just long enough to get experience on their resume, and then they move on to a network admin job with better pay and better hours."

"Well, that explains why people don't keep the job, but why wouldn't lots of people want the job? Just to get started? Just to get their foot in the door? I mean, I have no computer experience whatsoever, why offer me the job?"

"Good question. I guess it's just a matter of who's willing to put up with this shit long enough to get something out of it." Jeff grinned at me. "Are you?"

Jeff showed me around the call center, which had a big row of binders along the shelf that was built in, workstation height and depth, along the length of the wall. On the shelf were several phones, a lot of laptops, Ethernet cables poking out everywhere, one stray boxy PC, and piles of software CDs strewn everywhere. There was also a standalone printer/copy/fax, a couple of recycling bins overflowing with paper and empty Mountain Dew cans, a trash can stuffed with empty takeout food bags, and a bicycle propped against the wall. Also prominent in the room was a wall-mounted plasma TV, turned on to CNN.

"What's with the TV?" I asked.

"Calls can be unpredictable." Jeff grimaced. "Sometimes it's really busy, but some nights nobody calls for hours on end. We used to just surf the Internet, until we all found that it had an end, and we didn't like that end. So now, we have the TV on."

Jeff then took me for a walk through the server room. The server room felt like it was a brisk 42 degrees. The room was filled with aisles of metal shelves, stacked from bottom to top with blinking computer boxes. Bundles of cables ran into the back of all of the boxes. Lots of fun. In the middle of the room, a lone monitor stood on a shelf, plugged into a box, with a keyboard on a shelf below. "Wow, it's really cold in here," I remarked.

"Yeah, we have so many machines in here that if we don't keep the air turned on, the boxes will overheat and fry. So, it's heavily climate controlled in here. We all keep our drinks in here to keep them cold." Jeff gestured in the corner where there was a pile of Mountain Dew 12-packs stacked up, 3 or 4 packs high and deep. "We're not supposed to have food or drink in here, so don't open any up in here."

"Ok," I said. Jeff led me back to the call center, set me up with an account, and gave me the passwords to the admin accounts. I shadowed him as he took a couple of calls, watching which binders he used to find information to help the callers. After a while, Jeff asked, "Are you ready to take a call?" He had me take the next couple of calls. The user problems seemed fairly straightforward. Take the login, determine what level of support the caller had paid for, and proceed with gathering information on the caller's problems. "You're doing awesome. I'm going to hit the head. Cover any calls that come in." Jeff gestured at the phone, and then excused himself to the bathroom. A minute later, the phone began to ring.

"Thank you for calling MetroHiTek, this is Danny, how can I help you?" I stated.

"Hi," a female voice responded. "I'm locked out of my account, can you help me to reset my password?"

"Sure, can you give me your login ID?" I responded. She gave me her ID and I punched up her account on the computer. Linda Frahley, in Falls Church, Virginia. "Hi Ms. Frahley, are you still in Falls Church?"

The caller confirmed that she was.

"And can I have a number where I can reach you if we get disconnected?"

She rattled off her home number. It matched the number listed on the account, and the number on the caller ID on my phone.

"I notice that you have a basic account with us, so this support call with cost you $4.95 if you want to proceed. Do you want to proceed with the call?"

"What? Are you kidding? When I signed up for this account, the offer was all calls to IT were free."

I flipped through the binder to the customer contracts page. "Yes, the call is free, but the support is not. If you want to upgrade, for an added $15.95 per month, you get unlimited tech support. Otherwise, it's $4.95 each time you request support. Would you like to proceed with the call?"

Linda called me a couple of choice names, then huffily agreed to pay the $4.95. "I can't believe I can't remember my password. I only have so many pets and kids, after all."

I cringed. Even I knew that you shouldn't use your pet's name for a password. "Ma'am, can I get a credit card number from you to proceed with this transaction?"

"Sure, it's a Mastercard?" she offered, then rattled of a long number and an expiration date. I punched it in to the computer.

"And is it your name on the Mastercard account?" I asked.

"No," she responded, and then gave me a different name. I stared at the number on the screen. Something was ticking in my brain. Mastercard.

"Hey, can you reset the password?" the caller nagged.

"Sure..." I delayed. "Um, bear with me. I'm new to the job." I reset her password, but didn't give it to her yet. I logged into her account. The first four e-mails all appeared to be confirmation e-mails for gift card purchases. I clicked open the first one. "Hang on ma'am, just flipping through the binder." The e-mail showed a thousand dollar purchase of a gift card for a major retailer, shipped to a P.O. box, and ordered with a Visa card ending 4244. I toggled back to the screen where I'd input her payment. Mastercard. Ending 2777. HOLY SHIT. It matched the number that I had hacked onto my wall. I had stared at those ugly four digits every morning for days now. "Hang on ma'am, I'm just going to ask my supervisor if I'm doing this right, and then I'll get your password reset."

"ARGH you're going to put me on hold aren't you, you son of a bitch, don't put me on hold…!" she screeched, as I punched the hold button. What the hell could she do about it? She was locked out, and I had reset her password to one that she would never guess. She could stay on hold for a minute. Jeff walked back in.

"Hey man, how's it going?" he asked.

"Ok, I've got a customer on hold. I just wanted to ask you—if someone has an e-mail on our system, but they delete it, can we get it back?"

"Did she lose e-mail?"

"No, I'm just curious. Do we somehow have a way to recover that stuff?"

"Sure. We run taped backups every night, so as long as it's not hard-deleted the same day the e-mail was received, we can recover it."

"Awesome!" I punched back into the call, and said, "Ma'am? Your password is reset. 12345. Don't forget to reset it when you log back into your account, to something that you will remember but others won't forget."

"Yeah thanks," Linda said, then hung up on me. I jumped up, and punched my fist in the air.

"Woo hoo!" I screamed. "I got her! She is going to JAIL!" I dashed into the server room and grabbed a Mountain Dew, then jumped and kicked my feet in the air. "YES!" I landed too close to the stack of Mountain Dews, and accidentally kicked one with my foot. It flew across the room and hit the server rack. I stopped short and stared in horror as the can exploded, then landed on the ground and slowly began to bubble. My breath stopped, and then I realized that the soda was not going to spray on the servers. Instead, it just dripped out of the can and bubbled on the floor. I breathed a sigh of relief. Jeff wandered in.

"What the fuck, man? What's going on?" He looked in horror at the dripping can.

"A little accident, but it's ok," I said. "It's dripping on the floor, not on the servers."

"NO!" Jeff screamed. "That's a raised floor. All of the power cabling runs under the panels!" A dripping sound indicated that the Mountain Dew was dripping down into the crawlspace below the raised floor. "Shit!"

Crackling, popping sounds began under the floor. Smoke began to rise up, and the lights flickered. POP! The breaker switches tripped, and the power went out.

Oh, damn. Double damn. "Jeff?"

"Yeah man?"

"Do we need to get out of here?"

"Probably a good idea, just in case there's a teeny-tiny fire under there."

We regrouped in the parking lot. Jeff called his boss, and then the fire trucks showed up, followed by the fire marshall. I slunk down low, hoping he wouldn't recognized me from Ronald's boat. "Hey Jeff, if there was new data on those servers, is there any way to retrieve that information?"

"The whole server room just abruptly lost power without any of the servers being properly shut down. Not if there was new data that came in since the last backup. Any new e-mails, or whatever, that came in since last night midnight. It's 10:30, so that's over 22 hours of data that we lost."

"Damn." I stared at the building. My dumb ass had likely just erased the e-mail proving who the credit card thief was. Linda had just ordered those gift cards today using the stolen Visa card, and had given me the stolen Mastercard number to pay for her IT support. Electronic evidence of both transactions had just been erased from those servers by my impulsive actions. Why hadn't I just hit print and gotten a paper trail? I guess if I called the tip-line that Amaya had given me, I could give them the information. The credit card companies could follow up with the retailers that sold the gift cards. They should have evidence of the transaction. Maybe that would be good enough.

"Jeff, I'm sorry about this. Is this going to cost a lot of money? Clearly I'm fired.."

"To tell you the truth, we're off-shoring our help desk operation and migrating all of the server function to a data center in Texas. In a few weeks, all of these calls were supposed start routing through a call center in India. Our help desk guys found out, and they all quit and got new jobs. We don't have much of a staff right now, and we're having a harder time than ever trying to get folks to cover the phones. That's why we picked you up. These servers were going offline in a couple of weeks anyway. They'll probably just start the off-shore support a few weeks early now. Don't worry about this. Nobody will be local for MetroHiTek in three weeks. Just put us down as a reference, use my name, and lie your head off. Maybe you'll get another IT job."

Great, one night reading out of a binder and one major screwup causing total electronic failure and irrecoverable data loss. That and a plane ticket to India might get me a job.

Chapter THIRTEEN

I went home and crashed into bed, sleeping away most of Friday. I got up and showered late Friday afternoon. Initially the shower was pleasant, but abruptly the hot water broke off and I was drenched in an icy-cold spray. I screamed, slammed off the tap, and toweled off. What the hell? I absentmindedly dressed and headed out the door. The sun was getting low in the sky. I got into my car and started to cruise around. Traffic was heavy. I didn't really know what to do. I was out of steam—couldn't see going back to DOES, applying to a new job, trying again only to fail again. I drove aimlessly around the city. No point in going home to a house that was out of commission. No use in going to my brother's place. No room at my mother's house. No desire to go to my dad's. As I drove, my mind rolled over the total failure that my life had become, and I wondered what had happened. How did I get here? After a while, I realized that I was driving north, on the I-95, almost to Baltimore. Oh, what the hell. I took the

Baltimore beltway headed northwest, and got off at Reisterstown Road. A few twists and turns, and there I was by my sister's house.

My sister, Rachel, might be the only person in my family who is really good. Despite all the turmoil that we grew up in, she remained a calm and steady person, followed a good moral compass, and actually developed a spiritual life. She became religious as a teenager, and went to Israel for a year to attend a girls' seminary program. Now, she is married to a guy who, similarly, grew up in Reform Jewish home but became more religious as an adult. She teaches math at a Jewish private school, and he is in the middle of a medical residency. They have two small children, a baby, and choose to live in a tiny duplex in a very religious neighborhood.

Pimlico Racetrack, home of the Belmont, third race in the Triple Crown, abuts her neighborhood. The neighborhood itself struggles. It is the border between a stable, middle-class neighborhood and a grim, crime-ridden zone. Local community organizations offer various incentives to try to get families to move into the slowly expanding buffer zone, pushing the border between good and evil further and further out. Tensions occasionally flared between the families in the buffer zone and the denizens of the crime zone. As a result, the community still has to pitch in to shore up some of the services that I take for granted in my neighborhood, such as ambulance assistance or security patrol.

Tonight, as I stared out at her house, I realized that Rachel might not be home. It was Friday night, the Jewish Sabbath, and I didn't know if she was at synagogue or not. Men in black hats were beginning to fill the sidewalks, though, ambling home to their dinners, chatting and shaking hands goodbye. I don't know why they were walking so slowly. God knows, if I had a wife at home waiting with platters full of gefilte fish, pots filled with matzo ball soup, and warm baked chicken in the oven, I would be running, not walking, to get home. In houses all through this neighborhood, men were walking into their homes, blessing their children, chanting Hebrew prayers over over-flowing cups of wine, and passing around fresh slices of soft-warm challah bread. Why wasn't I? My chest and throat tightened a little, reflecting on the life these men were living that I had rejected. Their beautiful wives, perhaps in a wig or maybe a snood, wearing pearl necklaces and little diamond rings, lit Sabbath candles in tall silver candlesticks, warm lights to welcome them home. Later, they would put their children to bed and join together as husband and wife. I felt more lonely than ever.

Someone tapped on my window. I looked out to see two orthodox Jewish men looking seriously at me. I unrolled my window. "Yes?" I asked.

"Excuse me. We're with Shomrim. The neighborhood watch. Look, we look out for criminals here. We don't want any trouble. But you can't hang around like this. You have a strange car. You don't look like you belong here. Most folks in this neighborhood don't get drive-up visitors at this time on a Shabbos."

Shabbos. The Yiddish name for the Jewish Sabbath day, or Shabbat in Hebrew. I hadn't heard anyone say "Shabbos" in forever. I noticed that the guy who had done the talking was swallowing convulsively and shaking just slightly. He was a short, slim man. I reflected that he must be very serious about protecting his neighborhood. He looked like just about anyone could kick his ass, but he was still willing to confront a stranger and ask him to leave. I couldn't leave the poor guy in fear.

"Um, my sister lives here. Rachel. Rachel Stone," I said. "She isn't expecting me, I came without calling first. I mean, she wouldn't answer even if I called. Not tonight, that is. Not on Shabbos." God, I was babbling on. How could I explain to them that this woman who they likely knew as a pious and proper Jew had such a disaster for a brother?

"Well, are you going in? You can't hang around all night in the car, is what we're saying. And if you are Jewish, well, we'd prefer if you don't drive on Shabbos, if you know what I mean."

Ah, yes. Here it was. The morality police. These guys wouldn't do a lot of things on the jewish Sabbath, from Friday sundown to Saturday sundown, including work, turn on a light, turn off a light, make a phone call, or drive a car. They didn't want any other Jew to do so, either. It violates the jewish laws for observing the Sabbath, and keeps the messiah from coming. So forget that I had already driven up to town, they wouldn't want me to drive any further. In essence, I was stuck, because it wasn't unknown in this neighborhood for air to be let out of a tire just to keep someone from breaking the Sabbath. Maybe I should just drive off fast now, tires squealing, and get back to Virginia. On the other hand, if my car sat here all night and day until Saturday night when Shabbos ended, perhaps someone would steal it and relieve me of the hell of driving the enema car. At the thought that my car might end up in a chop shop very soon, I perked up, and hopped out. "Thank you," I said to the men, shaking their hands. "Good Shabbos, good Shabbos. Thank you so much, you have made a big difference in my life. You have no idea."

Smiling, I walked up to Rachel's house and knocked on the door. I could hear her shoes click on the hard wood floor of the foyer, and then a pause as she peeked through the peephole. Obviously if she was expecting company for dinner, they would be coming home with her husband, Aharon. She opened the door wide, a baby on her hip, a toddler clinging to her skirt.

"Danny, come in! Good Shabbos!" she cried. "It's so good to see you, I didn't know you were coming up!"

"I hope it's okay. I would have called but, you know..." I trailed off, twiddling my cell phone.

"Oh, it's okay, you are always welcome, come in!" Rachel said.

When we were growing up, life was crazy and stressful. My siblings and I all had our own ways of rebelling against our parents and differentiating our adult selves from our parents. My brother, Jason, became a brutal entrepreneur and made a sick amount of money. I went to graduate school and pursued a relentlessly shallow life of financial security and uber-respectability. Rachel rebelled by developing a deep and meaningful spiritual life, marrying a nice man and raising happy children, and getting a socially responsible job that brought benefit to the broader community. When we were teenagers, Rachel applied for a scholarship that let her spend a year of high school at a girls' seminary in Israel. When she returned home, she had traded her Levis for long skirts, tank tops for turtlenecks, and dates with boys for telephone study sessions on Torah learning. She got a part-time job three afternoons a week, and spent the money buying a little set of dishes, a minifridge, and a hotplate. On this set-up, she

cooked her own food so that she could keep kosher while still

living with the family. My mother was really agitated by all of

this change for a while, and would periodically yell and scream

at Rachel, berating her for getting "brainwashed" and worse.

To Rachel's credit, she never screamed back—just quietly

listened every time, then hugged Mom and gave her a big, "I

love you."

Rachel ended up furthering her lifestyle change by

winning a full scholarship to Stern College. While majoring in

education, she continued to remain date-free until her final

semester, when she went on three platonic dates with Aharon,

then a medical student at Albert Einstein Medical School, and

then got engaged. Aharon was also a baal teshuva, originally a

secular jew who became religious. Baal teshuva is sort of the

jewish version of becoming born again. Rachel and Aharon

were married two months later, and relocated down to

Baltimore when Aharon started his residency at Sinai Hospital in Baltimore. The upside of the hospital location, apparently, was that it was walking distance to the orthodox jewish neighborhood, so if Aharon had to do a shift that ended on Friday evening, he could walk home. I shuddered at the thought of anyone walking after dark in this neighborhood, but there you are. Rachel got a job teaching at the Bais Yaakov girls' school, and proceeded to have a series of closely-spaced babies that were all fortuitously born right at the start of summer break, resulting in perpetual employment with no loss of time for maternity leave.

Rachel led me through the foyer, cluttered with baby stroller, jackets, umbrella stand, and dropped Lego pieces, and into the living area. "Aharon will be home in about twenty minutes, so we can talk. Are you staying all of Shabbos? I'll make you up a bed. Let me set you a plate." Her home met all of my car reverie's expectations. Peeking into the dining room, I could see the table was covered with a soft pretty cloth, roses set in a crystal bowl in the center, and china dishes set around at each place setting, surrounded by silver cutlery and nicely pressed napkins. On the polished mahogany sideboard, tall silver candlesticks were lit with 4 inch tapers. The smell of fresh-baked bread and chicken soup drifted out of the kitchen. After setting an added place setting, Rachel joined me in the living room. I sat on the floral sofa, and she sat in an aging, second-hand velvet-upholstered wingback chair.

"So Danny, how are you? How is everything going?" Rachel smiled at me. I looked at her. Her face was soft and pretty, just as it had been when we were younger. She had always had long, shiny brown hair, but now it was pulled back out of view under a stretchy purple snood, embroidered with a few flowers. Little crystal beads and sequins accented the centers of the flowers. I guess a little bit of Mom's DNA had snuck into her, after all. Pearl earrings on her earlobes peeked out from the edge of the snood. Rachel was dressed in a high-necked, long-sleeved robe—the infamous Shabbos robe of the orthodox community. The toddler sat on the floor, playing with blocks, and the baby gurgled and pulled at Rachel's robe. The whole exterior was foreign to me, with the exception of Rachel's face.

"Oh, you know. Could be better. Hanging in there," I dutifully reported. "I've missed you. How are you?"

"We're doing well, thank God," Rachel responded. Thank God. The mantra of the religious. I wasn't sure if everything was going well because they thanked God all the time, or if they thanked God because it was all so good. "Aharon's residency is almost over, and he's going to go into practice. We're very excited. The children are all doing so well. And I'm working with a really neat group of girls this year. It's all good. And, B'sha Tova, I'm expecting again in a few months."

I looked at Rachel's stomach. I had missed it earlier, probably due to the flowing volume of the Shabbos robe, but sure enough, there was a round bubble poking out in her lap. "Wow," I said. "Is this your fourth baby?"

"Thank God!" she said. There it was again. "But Danny, really, how are you? Sound's like life has been a little rough for you lately. How are you doing?"

I wasn't really sure where to start. "Life is hard right now. Maybe I deserve it because I'm a sinner or whatever." I stopped, then started again. "I'm sure you don't approve of the way I live, but I can't do what you do. I'm not good at prayer. I'm not a good person." I stared at my hands. "Rachel, I'm not sure what to say to you."

Rachel was a little taken aback. "Danny. I don't think of you as a sinner. Why would you say that?"

It was clear that her feelings were hurt. I grunted uncomfortably, and shifted a little. "You know, I don't go to synagogue or pray much, and, um."

"Danny, I don't judge you. Nobody should judge. I made my choice of how to live, and you make your choice of how to live. I think it would be great if you pray, because I think it might improve your relationship with God, but that's YOUR relationship, not mine, and you have to build it in your own time."

I stared at her bookcase. It was an IKEA pressed-wood special, stretched from floor to ceiling next to the fireplace. The tallest top shelf were packed with tall volumes that had Hebrew titles that I couldn't read. Shelves below that were stuffed with books on Judaism—prayer books, learning books, biographies of great rabbis' lives, collections of letters from great rabbis, the Hitchhikers' Guide to the Galaxy. What?

"Rachel—did you know that you have Douglas Adams on your shelf?" I asked.

"Of course. I like Douglas Adams," she replied.

"But isn't that... unholy?"

Rachel laughed. "Danny, I'm a human being, not a religious robot. Please, think of me as the same person that you knew growing up, just dressed more modestly and a little more busy because I've worked in prayer a few times a day. That doesn't mean that I've gotten a lobotomy. Now come on, how are you? Tell me what you are really feeling." I had a sudden flashback to twelve-year old Rachel, in cut-offs over her tank style swimsuit, punching me in the stomach because I had licked her fudgsicle. I felt more at ease. This was my sister, after all.

"Life is just a fucking rat race!" I exploded. "We're just like little lab rats, running around and pressing the bar for pellets. We run the little races so that every two weeks we get the money pellets, and we keep doing it until we get enough money to check out like Lacey did, or until we die, whichever comes first. I don't know what to do. I can't figure out how to take a step back, how to process what has happened. Every day I'm rushing around, desperate to get a job, to get some money, to figure out how I'm going to make it to the next day. I feel like I need a day off from being unemployed. Does that sound crazy?" Rachel's toddler dropped some slobbery blocks and stared at me.

Rachel listened carefully and patiently as I rambled on. "Danny, it doesn't sound crazy at all. It sounds like you're trying to deal with a lot. You've suffered a lot of loss over the past few months. Your wife, your job—these are a big deal."

"It's not like anyone's died or anything," I mumbled.

"Still, these are the things that gave you a structure and a purpose to your life. Did you ever take time to grieve the loss of your marriage?"

"Oh, I don't miss Lacey. I'm over it."

"I'm talking about grieving for the loss of your relationship. You had expectations for your marriage. You were dedicated to it. Did you take time to mourn it?"

I'm not sure how a person could mourn over divorce; I certainly had not. "No. I'm sure I didn't. But she wasn't jewish, so mom says..."

"So what? She was your WIFE. You are allowed to miss her and be sad that it didn't work out. You loved her, right?"

"Yes." I sniffed. I closed my eyes. Tears welled up. I pressed my fingers to my eyelids. Slowly I shared with Rachel what I had learned the previous weekend about my ex-wife and our sham marriage.

"Oh, honey." Rachel gave me a sympathetic look, and handed me a kleenex. "That is really heavy stuff. There's so much rejection and withholding packed into the situation. Not knowing about your wife's pregnancies? Being rejected as a spouse and a sexual partner. And all on top of everything else that has happened to you. Did you consider talking to a therapist?"

"Are you kidding? I didn't consider that until after I lost my job, and at that point, I couldn't afford to. All of my benefits were through work. With no money and no health insurance, I couldn't go talk to someone for $150 an hour."

"Wow, it sounds like this is very hard on you, with no outlet. No friends to discuss with?"

"Friends—ha, they scattered to the four winds. I have nothing. You know, I had one life insurance policy that was a stand-alone policy, not through work. The policy was for $2 million. It was due to be renewed a couple of days ago. The day before it expired, I cried. I knew I couldn't write a check to pay the policy. I couldn't afford it. I sat there and thought, I have no wife. I have no children. Aside from this policy, I have no money. I just have a giant debt on a sinking hole of a house. If I died, there would be no evidence of me left on the world. I seriously considered committing suicide. I sat there with the gun in my hand, and cried. What did I add to the world?"

"What happened?" Rachel asked softly. "What kept you with us?"

"I remembered that Lacey was still the beneficiary on the policy. There was no way in hell I was going to eat a bullet and make her one penny richer. I held the gun until the stroke of midnight, when the policy expired, and then I let it go and went to bed." I laughed a little at the awfulness of my story. Rachel smiled a little.

"I'm glad you are still here. We love you, and you will get past all of this. Even if you can't afford to pay a therapist, you can speak with me, you can meditate, you can funnel your frustrations in other creative ways. You'll see, there are ways to process these life events to gain knowledge and wisdom."

"Like what?"

"Well, why don't you just write it all down in a book? Journaling can be very therapeutic."

The door swung open, and Aharon walked in along with his daughter and another couple that he had invited over for Shabbos dinner. Rachel and Aharon introduced me to their guests and we shook hands all around. I sat down at the table and listened as the men sang Hebrew songs. Then Aharon poured the wine and chanted Kiddush over the wine. We all

drank, and then washed for challah. The soft, warm Shabbos

challah was sweet and delicious. Aharon poured out more

wine for all of the adults. My little niece and nephew had

sippy cups of juice. The baby dropped his bottle over the side

of his high chair and screamed. I leaned over to retrieve it for

him, and the smiled, giggled, and dropped it again. Scream!

Then, Rachel brought out dish after dish of savory, Shabbos

food. We all stuffed ourselves with Gefilte fish, horseradish,

and salad, followed by matzo ball soup, then roast chicken,

potato kugel, and green beans. Aharon offered around L'chaim

and we all toasted and drank shots. Rachel followed up with a

choice of desserts—spicy cinnamon walnut bundt cake, and

peanut butter pie.

Dessert was followed with bentching—the grace after

meal. I sang along for the first few paragraphs, then trailed

off into "nhur nhur nhur..." as the prayer kept going and

going. My niece, Aviva, wandered over with some battered

looking story books. "Uncle Danny, will you read me a story?" she asked. I looked over at Rachel, and she kept singing the prayers but nodded and smiled at me. I gratefully escaped the table and went back over to the couch, where Aviva and I snuggled up and read Dr. Suess. After the guests left, Rachel hustled the kids into their jammies and bed. Then, she showed me into the guest room, and left me to my thoughts.

I woke early the next morning, and decided to leave. Rachel and Aharon would want me to stay for the whole Shabbos, but I had no clothes that were appropriate to wear to synagogue, and thought it would be a little awkward if I just hung around the house all day, especially with my embarrassing car in front of the house. I quietly snuck out the front door, and saw that my car had survived all night without any further damage. I slid into the driver's seat, turned over the engine, and made my way back down to Northern Virginia.

I felt good. Energized. Everything was looking up. Nothing was different, but everything was better. I remembered Rachel's advice—just write it all down. I found a

CVS and ran in. Aisle six had notebooks on sale, 2 for $3. I

grabbed a couple, took them home, and started writing. I got it

all down, everything that had happened to me up until now.

Thanks for reading it.

* * * *

The editor's foot dropped on the floor. He looked again at the

clock. 11:19 at night. His office light was on, but all of the

other offices were dark, and the hallway was dark. He smiled,

and tucked the notebook into his ACCEPT pile. *Fuck real*

estate, he thought.

About the Author: Sara Logan lives outside of Washington DC with her husband and her three sons. She has a full-time job, a boring car, and is up-to-date on her mortgage.

Acknowledgements: Many thanks to Mary DuRousseau and Shiera BenDov for reading and commenting on early drafts of this novel. Thank you to my wonderful husband, Miles, for taking care of everything while I found time to write. Finally, thank you to my family for all of their love and support.

www.ingramcontent.com/pod-product-compliance
Lightning Source LLC
Chambersburg PA
CBHW071300170626
46809CB00001B/291